A KISS FOR MISS FRAZER

"If you are concerned that I do not possess the romantic skills of your rake, let me assure you that while my experience may not be as vast as his, my wish to please you is far greater."

Her breath seemed oddly elusive. "But you do not desire to kiss me."

Not desire to kiss her? Heaven have mercy. Now he knew she was mad.

Against his better judgment, his gaze swept over her reclined form. With her hair spilling like satin fire over the crisp white pillows and her eyes darkened with emotion, she appeared as delectable as the most experienced temptress.

"That is perhaps the most ridiculous thing I have ever heard," he rasped, his heart jolting against his chest. "I have ached to kiss you since the moment I arrived in London."

"You are merely saying that to confuse me."

Luce growled deep in his throat, slowly lowering his head toward the temptation of her lips.

Obviously, she needed proof of his sincerity . . .

BOOKS BY DEBBIE RALEIGH

Lord Carlton's Courtship

Lord Mumford's Minx

A Bride for Lord Challmond

A Bride for Lord Wickton

A Bride for Lord Brasleigh

The Christmas Wish

The Valentine Wish

The Wedding Wish

A Proper Marriage

A Convenient Marriage

A Scandalous Marriage

My Lord Vampire

My Lord Eternity

My Lord Immortality

Miss Frazer's Adventure

Published by Zebra Books

Miss Frazer's Adventure

Debbie Raleigh

ZEBRA BOOKS
Kensington Publishing Corp.
www.kensingtonbooks.com

PROLOGUE

As far as weddings went, the wedding between Lucius Jonathon Duval, Earl of Calfield, and Miss Katherine Frazer could be considered an extravagant, spectacular . . . failure.

Oh, the blame could not be attributed to the small church, despite its being crammed to the rafters by the crush of elegant guests. Nor upon the bride, who stood at the altar with her countenance nearly as pale as the ivory dress she had chosen for the solemn occasion. Nor even upon the vicar, who had obviously imbibed heavily from the silver flask he kept concealed beneath his robes.

Weddings by tradition included overcrowded churches, pale brides, and vicars who felt the need to succor their nerves with a swig of brandy.

No. The disaster could be attributed entirely to the groom.

A groom who had never bothered to make his appearance . . .

CHAPTER ONE

Four hours after being abandoned at the altar, Kate Frazer paced through her bedchamber.

It was a beautiful room. A spacious affair that her father had commanded thoroughly refurbished when he had purchased the estate five years before. Drenched in pale blue and ivory, it boasted a magnificent view of the Kent countryside and the rarified scent of pure wealth. A perfect setting for the proper, dutiful daughter of Sir Archibald Frazer.

Today, however, Kate took little notice of how her satin slippers sank into the floral carpet. Or how the mullioned windows reflected the pale November sunlight.

Instead she battled the urge to hit something. Preferably the handsome countenance of her treacherous fiancé. Damn and blast Lucius Jonathon Duval, Lord of Calfield.

It had been bad enough to know that the man was merely marrying her for the vulgarly large dowry her father had offered. And that during their brief engagement, he had called upon her on less than a half dozen occasions, and then, she was convinced, only to ensure that she had not met an untimely end and deprived him of his windfall.

And now . . . this.

Reaching a small pier table that held a particularly

ugly collection of china figurines that had been an engagement gift from Lord Calfield's aunt, Kate was about to turn and resume her pacing when she abruptly halted. For a moment she glared at the hapless treasures. And then she did the unthinkable. Or at least the unthinkable for a maiden who was always proper, always dutiful, and always anxious to please others.

Plucking a delicate figurine from the table, she turned and launched it at the door.

Rather to her surprise, the sound of splintering china provided a distinct sense of satisfaction. Perhaps not as satisfying as tossing the projectiles at Calfield's golden head, but at the moment, she would take what she could get.

She reached for another figurine, then rapidly turned and tossed it in the same direction as the other. Before it could land, however, the door was suddenly thrust open and a tall, dark-haired maiden was forced to abruptly double over with a faint shriek.

"Kate?" Julia Alexander warily straightened to regard her with an expression that revealed her fear that Kate had plunged over the edge. "Are you . . . all right?"

Wryly, Kate glanced down at the ivory silk wedding gown that had cost her father a near fortune. "Oh, I am just splendid."

"You are certain?"

"Why would I not be?" She offered her young cousin a tight smile. "I absolutely adore devoting hours to having my hair wrenched into painful curls, my poor body poked, pushed, and prodded into a corset from the netherworld, and all so that I can stand before a hundred smugly amused strangers who are there to witness my spectacular humiliation."

Julia grimaced. "Forgive me, Kate. That was a ridiculous question, considering the circumstances."

Kate heaved a sigh. "No, I am the one who is sorry. I should not snap at you. This fiasco is certainly not your fault."

Her cousin stepped closer, her expression troubled. "Do you wish to talk about it?"

Kate shuddered, her arms wrapping across her heaving stomach. "Talk about what? I was jilted. There is little more to be said."

The lovely dark eyes that Kate had always secretly envied narrowed as Julia took another step closer.

"Are you so very certain?"

"I beg your pardon?"

"Are you certain that Lord Calfield intended to jilt you?"

Kate blinked, briefly wondering if her cousin had been sneaking into the numerous bottles of champagne her father had intended for the wedding breakfast. That could surely be her only excuse.

"I should think that was fairly obvious, Julia. A gentleman does not unintentionally jilt his bride," she retorted between gritted teeth. "He must make a decided effort to avoid the church where his presence is expected."

"Yes, but . . ." Julia frowned. "What if there was a reason he did not arrive at the church?"

"You fear he may have been captured by pirates? Or perhaps he tragically went mad and is even now roaming the countryside?"

"Of course not. But what if there was an accident?"

Kate's lips thinned at the mere suggestion. She might be overly naive for a woman of four and twenty years, but she was not an utter imbecile.

"Lord Calfield's estate is but two miles from the

church. Had there been an accident we would have known."

"Well then, perhaps he is ill."

"And not one of his servants could be bothered to carry a message to me? Really, Julia, you are grasping at straws. The truth is painfully obvious. He finally accepted that the glittering promise of a fat dowry was not worth wedding me."

Julia gave a shake of her head, her gaze briefly flickering over her cousin's tiny form. Kate knew precisely what she was seeing. A woman too short and slender to look anything but foolish in the elegant gown. Red hair that was ruthlessly tamed in a crown of curls and eyes that refused to be either blue or green. An awkward, plain dab of a woman who had never felt comfortable in her own skin.

"That cannot be true, Kate," she said softly.

"Why ever not?"

Julia drew in a harsh breath. "Because for all his faults, Lord Calfield is a gentleman."

A wry smile curved Kate's lips. "As were King Richard the Third and the Marquis de Sade. What does that have to do with the matter?"

"Everything, as you well know." A hint of impatience touched the pretty countenance. "He would not behave in such a dastardly fashion. Not at the risk of being condemned by society and leaving himself vulnerable to a breach of promise suit."

"Which only reveals how desperate he must have been."

"Oh, Kate." Julia gave a rueful shake of her head. "I think you should at least wait until you have spoken with the man before you condemn him as a heartless beast."

Kate offered an inelegant snort. She was not at all in the humor to offer Lord Calfield the benefit of the doubt. Not after standing for nearly an hour at that blasted altar listening to the giggles and snide comments whispered behind her back.

In truth, all she wanted was to forget that Lord Calfield even existed.

Blast it all. She had made an utter fool of herself, and for what?

For a fiancé who considered her no more than a nuisance necessary to acquiring a fortune? For a father who was desperate to thrust her onto the first willing gentleman? For her own sense of uncertainty?

Enough was enough.

Her entire life she had struggled to play the role of the perfect maiden. After her mother had abandoned the family for a charming, worthless rogue and taken herself off to Paris, it had been made painfully obvious that she was being constantly judged. From her father to the tenants, all had waited to determine if she had inherited more than her mother's red hair and slender form.

Bad blood ran in her veins, she was too often reminded, and it was her duty to prove she was capable of overcoming any wicked impulses.

Well, frankly, at the moment she was sick to bloody death of being the proper Miss Frazer.

She had done everything that was demanded of her. She had followed every rule. She had meekly submitted to the opinions of others. One day she was going to die, she told herself, and what would be her epitaph?

Here lies a pitiful, bitter old spinster who died alone in her cold bed with no one to mourn her passing.

The knowledge shook her to the very core.

"No, Julia. I have no interest in ever seeing Lord Calfield again. Even if he came to me with a thousand tragic excuses, I would not consent to marry him. Not after today."

Clearly startled by her cousin's uncharacteristic stubbornness, Julia gave a faint frown.

"You are naturally upset," she offered in comforting tones. "Once you have had the opportunity to contemplate . . ."

"I have contemplated," Kate interrupted in fierce tones, her eyes glittering with a hectic glow. "Perhaps for the first time in my life. And I will tell you that I have come to a few unpleasant truths about myself."

"What do you mean?"

Kate struggled to put her overwhelming sense of restless anger into words. "When I was forced to stand at that altar and consider my future, I realized that I had far too many regrets."

Julia lifted her hands in a sympathetic motion. "Any woman would feel betrayed, Kate."

"No, it was more than that," Kate insisted. "I suddenly realized that I have never truly been happy."

Julia gave a choked sound of surprise, glancing pointedly about the elegant chamber that would make the most demanding maiden drool.

"You must be jesting. You possess everything a woman could desire. Wealth, position, and a fiancé who makes maidens swoon in delight."

A month ago, Kate might have agreed. She was safe in her isolated world. As long as she behaved and did as she was told, there were no troubles, no fears, no disappointments.

And no pleasure, she realized. No excitement. No risks. None of the things that made life worthwhile.

"Julia, do you realize that I have never made a decision for myself?" Kate demanded, suddenly plagued by a sharp sense of restless energy. "For years I have allowed my father to utterly manage me. He chose my wardrobe, my friends, and what social functions I was allowed to attend. I was never consulted, or my opinion requested. Not even when it came to acquiring a husband."

Julia gave a sudden grimace. "Good gads, Kate, I have been warning you for years that you were far too biddable. But you always claimed that you were content. Even when your father announced your engagement, you assured me that it was what you desired."

"Because I allowed myself to be convinced it was for the best." Her features hardened in remembered disgust. "After all, I am the daughter of a scandalous, wicked jade. How could I possibly be trusted to choose what was expected of a respectable maiden? Now I realize that I have been a fool."

"No, not a fool," Julia softly breathed. "Just a dutiful daughter."

Kate abruptly tilted her chin. "Well, no more."

"I . . ." Julia suddenly regarded her in a wary manner. "What are you going to do?"

Kate stilled at the unexpected question.

What was she going to do?

After the most humiliating day in her life, did she intend to return to being the sweet, biddable Miss Kate Frazer?

No.

A warm rush of determination filled her body. She would not, could not, go back to the way things had been before.

She had been given a . . . what was the word? A revelation. One of those rare moments of clarity where the truth kicked you right in the head.

She was a different Kate Frazer.

A Kate who longed to break free of her tedious life. A Kate who would not be afraid of risks or of making her own decisions.

She was going to be bold and daring and free.

Just as her mother had been.

With a brilliant smile, she met her cousin's worried gaze squarely.

"I'm going to do . . . everything."

"Everything?"

"Everything I have missed," Kate announced, audaciously sweeping the rest of the figurines onto the floor as she paced to stare at the frosty Kent countryside. "I want to go to London and visit the theater. I want to see the Prince and ride through Hyde Park. I want to know what it is like to be cast to the wind and I want to have a glorious flirtation with some man I have no intention of marrying. I want to enjoy myself with no concern of what is proper."

There was a shocked silence before Julia gave a disbelieving laugh. "Good heavens, you have gone mad."

Kate slowly turned with a rueful grin. "Perhaps I have, but for the moment I do not care."

Her cousin studied her for a long moment, then a sudden smile eased her concern. "I was wrong. I think that at long last you have come to your senses. I could not be happier."

"Really?"

"Yes, really."

"Do you know . . . neither could I."

Julia's smile slightly dimmed. "Still, what of your father? He has always refused to allow you to go to London."

Kate's sense of euphoria briefly faded at the mention of her father. As Julia had pointed out, he had adamantly refused her timid requests for a London season. At the time, he had claimed that it was an utter waste of money, but they both knew it was his fear that she might cause him embarrassment that had kept her firmly imprisoned in the country.

"I shall tell him that I am visiting Aunt Clara to recover from my terrible disappointment," she retorted, refusing to admit even to herself that the thought of confronting her father was more than a little nerve-racking. "He will never know that I am instead traveling to London."

"And if your father hears rumors of you in London?" Julia demanded.

Kate slowly smiled. "He will not."

"How can you be so certain?"

"Because, Miss Kate Frazer shall not be in London."

"What?"

"From the moment I leave Kent, I shall be Mrs. Katherine Freemont. A lonely widow in dire need of a bit of adventure."

"Good God." Julia gave a slow shake of her head. "This has all the makings of a disaster."

Kate forced herself to give an indifferent shrug. Such worries were for tomorrow.

Today was a new beginning.

Tonight was the end.

His final night of freedom.

Sprawled comfortably upon the bed with nothing more than a pair of buckskins covering his lean, muscular form and his arm pillowing his golden head, Lord Calfield glanced about the cramped bedchamber of the Posting Inn.

It possessed little to recommend it.

The furnishings were shabby, the air filled with the stench of fried onions, and the sheets far less pristine than even the most tolerant patron would endure. It was also frequented by the sort of smugglers, ruffians, and pirates who were certain to maintain a boisterous mayhem well past decent hours.

Hardly the setting for a blue-blooded Peer of the Realm. But then, Luce was not at all a typical peer.

Taking a deep drink of the cheap red wine, he negligently passed the bottle to his grizzled companion.

"A toast, Foster," he drawled with a smile that revealed perfect white teeth that gleamed in the muted candlelight. "May your waters always be smooth, your ship steady, and the damnable Frenchies floundering upon the rocks."

"Hear, hear." With a flourish, the hardened sailor lifted the bottle and drank deeply of the wine. Once satisfied, he wiped his lips with the sleeve of his jacket and regarded Luce with a pair of shrewd blue eyes. "I must say, you do not appear particularly concerned for a man who has just missed his wedding."

"What would you have me do?" Luce's lips twisted with wry amusement. "I suppose I could have my spineless maggot of a captain drawn and quartered. It was, after all, because of his fussing and fretting over a few clouds that I was unable to return to Kent at the proper time."

"A few clouds?" Foster harrumphed in disgust. " 'Twas a raging storm. Only a madman would have set sail in such weather."

"Fah. You have become a persnickety old woman since I put you in command of the *Windsong*."

Foster gave a lift of his shoulder. "She's a beauty

of a ship. It would be a shame to have her at the bottom of the Channel."

"So instead, you have ensured that I am labeled a blackguard and scoundrel," Luce retorted dryly. "And no doubt condemned me to a tiresome raking over the coals by my prospective father-in-law."

Foster took another swig of wine before handing the bottle to Luce. "It wasn't my notion to linger in London until last evening. You were the one to insist that we had ample time before the wedding."

Wedding. His wedding. Taking a deep, rather desperate gulp of the wine, Luce suppressed a small shudder.

It was one thing to vaguely accept the notion that he was in dire need of a wealthy bride. It was quite another to realize he was mere hours from being forever shackled to a near stranger.

Still, what could he do?

After discovering the wretched mess his worthless father had made of the family fortune, he had to do something. And something swiftly. His own modest wealth had been tied up in the fleet of ships he had purchased over the past ten years, and while his enterprising efforts were beginning to show results, he in no way possessed the funds to haul his father's estate out of the mire of debt. And there was not a banker about who was willing to loan the necessary capital upon the risky promise of Luce's shipping profits.

That, of course, was when Sir Frazer had made his timely, or perhaps untimely, appearance.

Luce grimaced as he recalled the coarse, overly brash man who had bluntly offered to marry off his only daughter in exchange for a very large dowry. At first Luce had been horrified. He was no rank fortune hunter who would sell himself to the highest bidder. No matter how tempting that bid might be. Besides which, any daughter of such an uncouth lout was bound to be unbearable.

But then he had actually met Miss Frazer.

It had been a shock to discover that rather than the overblown shrew he had expected, she had proved to be a shy, retiring maiden who had regarded him with a startlingly intelligent gaze. And even more shocking had been the realization that he had felt a pang of sympathy for the poor girl.

It was obvious that she was hounded and browbeaten by her bully of a father. And that she would be made miserable if he chose to walk away and leave her to bear the brunt of Frazer's disappointment.

Suddenly, he began to wonder if wedding Miss Frazer would be such a horrid notion after all. She was clearly the sort of woman who would make a nice, sweet-tempered wife. One who would not be overly demanding nor inclined to complain when he was forced to concentrate upon his business.

And heaven knew that he would be more kind to her than her own father.

Why not? a devilish voice had whispered in the back of his mind. It would surely solve both their troubles.

And so, in a fit of madness, he had requested that she become his wife. He had always been a gambler. And a very successful gambler at that. Surely, choosing a wife was no different from throwing the dice and hoping for the best?

"I thought it best to finish my business before returning to Kent," he retorted in unconsciously defensive tones. "It would hardly do to abandon my bride mere hours after the wedding. Now, I am free to devote the next few weeks to her pleasure."

The ruddy, deeply lined countenance held a hint

of wry amusement. "Finish your business, eh? And perhaps enjoy a last taste of the lovely Maria?"

Luce smiled ruefully at the thought of the fiery redheaded courtesan who had been his mistress for the past year. The illegitimate daughter of a Spanish aristocrat, she had taken London by storm when she first arrived in England. It had been a shock to all when she had chosen Luce as her protector rather than one of the far more wealthy and powerful gentlemen who vied for her attention.

"A most tempting notion, you old lecher. However, I offered Maria her congé shortly after I requested that Miss Frazer become my wife. For all my faults, and I will admit they are numerous, I have no desire to follow in my father's less than honorable footsteps. Unless Miss Frazer denies me her bed, I will be faithful to her."

"Well, well." Seemingly startled by Luce's admission, Foster raised his brow. "That must have been quite an unpleasant surprise for dear Maria."

Luce gave a lift of his shoulder. "I will admit that she did not take the announcement with any amount of grace. But, I do not doubt that she had my replacement within her grasp before her pretty tears dried."

"No doubt." Foster regarded him for a long moment. "So now you must only hope that Miss Frazer has not decided to cry off."

"Cry off?" Luce offered a blink of surprise. "Why the devil would she cry off?"

"You did leave her stranded at the altar, Luce."

"An unavoidable accident." Luce briefly considered his meek, rather timid fiancée. "No doubt she will be disappointed, but once I explain, all will be well."

Foster tilted back his head to give a sudden, unexpected laugh at his perfectly logical words.

"Good gads, you surely are not that foolish?"

"What do you mean?"

"There isn't a woman born who wouldn't be infuriated beyond bearing at being jilted. You shall be fortunate if she doesn't shoot you on sight."

"Ridiculous." Luce settled himself more comfortably upon the mattress. "I did not jilt her. Besides, Miss Frazer is unlike most maidens. Which is precisely why I agreed to wed her. She is not temperamental, nor inclined to hysterics. Indeed, I doubt she possesses the spirit to even complain of my tardy arrival."

Foster gave a shake of his head. "I fear you are bound for an unpleasant surprise."

Luce shrugged, draining the last dregs of the wine before tossing the bottle onto the floor.

"Allow *me* to worry about my fiancée, Foster." He scrubbed his hands over his countenance, a heavy weariness clutching at his body. For days he had traced his way through the docks of London, ensuring his ships would be suitably filled with cargoes before he returned to Kent. Now he desired nothing more than several hours of uninterrupted sleep. "Perhaps you will forgive me, but I must have some rest before arriving at the church. It would never do for the bridegroom to fall asleep on his wedding night."

Foster rose to his feet with a loud snort. "If there is a wedding."

"Oh, there will be a wedding." Luce smiled with hard determination. "No matter what my feelings of being leg-shackled, I know my duty to my mother and sisters. As well as to my fiancée. If I must be sacrificed upon the altar, then that is exactly what will happen. Nothing will halt this marriage."

CHAPTER TWO

Kate was quite convinced that it would have been easier to tunnel her way to France than to secretly make her way to London. Her father's rigid supervision made it necessary to call in the assistance of both her devoted maid and Julia, as well as straining every bit of her imagination to ensure that nothing would alert Sir Frazer that anything was amiss.

Still, when Kate had arrived in London, she realized it had been worth every nerve-racking moment. She had no notion that it would prove to be just as exciting as she had always dreamed it would be.

Now, seated upon the bench situated in the tiny garden behind her hotel, she sucked in a deep breath. What could possibly be better? Busy days visiting the various museums and more notable sights, evenings devoted to the theater and intellectual salons.

Kent seemed far away.

Wonderfully, gloriously far away.

In truth, she had experienced more than a few doubts when she packed her bags and climbed into the coach bound for London.

Could her recent humiliation have unsettled her to the point where she was behaving irrationally?

Was she risking utter ruin to fulfill a handful of emotional impulses she did not even comprehend?

The answer had come to her the moment she arrived at the modest but tidy hotel.

Mad or not, she felt alive for perhaps the first time in her life.

There were no anxious efforts to please her father. No constant fear her every movement was being observed by her neighbors. No cowering behind the demure manner and retiring deference that was expected of her.

Instead, there was an addictive sense of independence. A sensation she could do anything and everything. And to effectively prove that the old Kate was gone forever, she had deliberately devoted her first days in the city to shopping for a dashing wardrobe that had nothing in common with her aging-spinster image.

A wardrobe that symbolized the daring, joyous woman she intended to become.

"A beautiful day, is it not?"

The husky, deliciously dark male voice brought Kate's head jerking upward. Her heart ricocheted about her chest as her gaze slowly traveled up the lean body attired in black breeches and a precisely cut green coat. She had a stunned impression of elegant muscles and a broad chest before her gaze at last reached the finely handsome features with a pair of raven black eyes.

Heaven have mercy.

He was every fantasy a maiden could harbor. A dream come to life with the features of an angel and the eyes of a devil. She struggled to recall how to breathe.

A wicked gleam of amusement entered those black eyes, and Kate abruptly realized that she was gaping at him like a landed trout. With a stern effort, she reminded herself that she was the new Kate.

This Kate did not cringe with the fear she was being judged and found wanting. She did not scurry to a distant corner and hope to be overlooked. She did not expect to be regarded with amused disdain.

This Kate could look any gentleman in the eye and not give a bloody damn what he thought.

"Any day that the sun condescends to make an appearance in England is a beautiful day," she quipped lightly. "Do you not think?"

He gave a smoky laugh. "Somehow it just became more beautiful. May I join you?"

Thoroughly shocked, Kate could think of nothing clever to say. "I . . . if you wish."

"Oh, I wish." With graceful ease, the stranger stretched himself onto the bench beside her. Shifting, he settled himself so that he could regard her with open interest. "Allow me to offer my introduction: I am Lord Thorpe. And you?"

Her days in London had prepared her for such a moment. There was not even a hesitation as she readily replied.

"Mrs. Freemont."

"Mrs.?" His gaze dropped to her bare fingers. "You are wed?"

"A widow."

"Ah." His smile deepened. "And recently arrived in London, unless I miss my guess."

Kate discovered herself regarding him with a hint of unease. Surely she could not be such an awkward country miss that she could be spotted at a hundred paces? Not after all her efforts to appear the sophisticated lady of Town.

"Why do you presume that I would be recently arrived?"

"Because our paths have not yet crossed. I never overlook a beautiful woman."

Beautiful?

Her?

She briefly wondered if this man might be a bit loony. Or perhaps merely foxed. She had often heard the female servants giggle over the notion that a gentleman would grope and grapple at anything in skirts when he was drinking.

Then she gave an inward shrug. What did it matter?

She was in London.

The sun was shining.

She was wearing a shimmering gown in a bold shade of crimson, with a lovely tailored spencer.

And a gorgeous, delectable rake was regarding her as if she were a tasty morsel rather than something he found stuck to the bottom of his boot.

"I see. Do you make a habit of crossing the paths of beautiful women?"

"But of course."

"And I presume that you have crossed a great number of paths?" she daringly murmured.

He gave a soft laugh. "A most dangerous question, my lovely Mrs. Freemont. In truth, there have not been near so many as the gossips would have you believe. What pleasure is there in the more mundane beauty? I possess an appreciation for only the most rare and unique treasures."

Her heart gave a faint flutter. A rake, indeed.

"Very pretty."

"As are you." His gaze warmly stroked her features. "Are you a guest of the hotel?"

"For the moment. Are you staying here as well?"

"Unfortunately, no. I possess a town house in Mayfair."

"Oh." She tilted her head to one side. "Is this not a private garden for guests of the hotel only?"

The dark eyes gleamed with amusement. "You are not going to call for the authorities, are you?" he protested. "This is one of the loveliest gardens in all of London."

"Hmm . . ."

"I throw myself on your mercy."

She pretended to consider his transgression. "I do not know. It is the rules, after all."

"I detest rules. Besides, I have the perfect solution."

Feeling a thrill of excitement that she had never experienced before, Kate gave a small smile.

"And what is that?"

He deliberately leaned forward. "You allow me to remain, and I promise to escort you to all the sights and entertainments that London has to offer."

She wrinkled her nose. "But I have already visited most of the famous sights and attended the theater."

"Fah. I do not refer to such tedious diversions," he chided softly. "You must be in the company of a gentleman who has an intimate knowledge of the city to discover the hidden enjoyments."

Although determined to be reckless and daring, Kate was not stupid. At least not that stupid.

"A most tempting offer, but surely you do not presume that I would allow an unknown gentleman to escort me about London?"

"Perhaps not," he conceded with a grin. "The obvious solution is for us to become better acquainted. Then when you ride off in my carriage, it will not be with a stranger."

Kate gave a reluctant laugh at his persistence. She suddenly realized she had never experienced such sensations. Giddy, frightened, and utterly amazed, all rolled into one.

"You must be vastly attached to this garden."

The dark eyes stroked over her slender form. "I am becoming more attached by the moment."

A pleasant tingle feathered over her skin at his lingering gaze. This gentleman was making it very easy to pretend she was the sort of beautiful, charming woman who could attract a handsome man's attention.

Scouring her brain for some brilliant retort, Kate was suddenly wrenched from her pleasant haze as a dark shadow fell across the bench.

A shiver of premonition raced through her, even as she told herself that she was being ridiculous. There was nothing to fear. It was no doubt a passing servant. Or another guest who was drawn to the beautiful garden just as she had been.

Slowly, almost reluctantly, she lifted her head. For a moment, the bright afternoon sunlight blinded her and all she could make out was a shadowed figure of a man. Then her breath caught in disbelief.

No. It could not be.

Lord Calfield. Here. In London. In her private, wonderful garden.

Just like the deceitful, slimy snake in the Garden of Eden.

A swift, undeniable fury swept through her as her gaze clashed with the startling blue eyes.

Attired in buff breeches and blue coat, he appeared as frightening as a Nordic god. Proud, determined, and fiercely ruthless beneath his smooth charm. Not a rake, but a conqueror who would sweep all from his path with an iron will.

Offering a hard smile, he thrust a hand through the hair that shimmered like golden silk beneath the sunlight.

"Well, my dear Kate, I do hope you are pleased with yourself. You have led me upon quite a merry chase."

"You," she breathed in low tones.

He arched an arrogant brow. "Yes. Surely you are not surprised to see me?"

"Surprised" was not the word she would use, Kate seethed. Angry, horrified, and even outright livid would be closer to the emotions boiling through her.

"How did you find me?" she demanded without preamble, although it was a ridiculous question. This gentleman possessed the sort of cunning intelligence that could have tracked her to a cave in the netherworld.

He gave a shrug. "I will admit that it was not an easy task. You covered your tracks unexpectedly well. Thankfully, you were recognized at the Posting Inn and I was able to follow you to London. Of course, I was then forced to search through every lodging house and hotel until I managed to locate you. A tedious task, and one, I must warn you, that has left me in a rather foul mood."

No doubt, if Kate possessed a lick of sense, she would be terrified of his smoldering impatience. He was large and dangerous and obviously ready to throttle her.

Her good sense, however, had thankfully been left in Kent, and rather than fearing her fiancé, she battled the urge to box his ears.

He was going to ruin everything.

"I must say, my lord, that I am all amazement." She flashed a defiant smile. "You made it painfully

obvious in Kent that you would go to great lengths
to avoid my companionship. Even to the point of
humiliating me before the entire county. Why ever
would you make such a belated effort now?"

He stiffened at her cold rebuff, clearly startled
that the timid mouse would dare to do anything
but whimper for forgiveness beneath his displea-
sure.

"You are mistaken, Kate. I did not intention-
ally avoid your companionship. My delay was
unavoidable."

Ah. So he had come to regret tossing away his
lovely fortune. And now he thought he had only
to snap his fingers to have her eagerly scurrying to
be his unfortunate but necessary burden of wealth.

"Is that so?"

"Yes." He folded his arms over his chest as he
peered down the length of his arrogant nose. "I had
every intention of fulfilling my duty. As you would
have discovered if you had not so foolishly chosen to
disappear rather than await my explanation."

"Oh yes, I am quite certain you have any number
of excuses at your fingertips, my lord. Unfortunately, I no longer care to hear them."

"No longer care to hear them?" His brow fur-
rowed. "What the devil does that mean?"

Her features unconsciously hardened. "The past
is behind me. I intend to concentrate only on the
present. A present that was quite delightful until
you made an appearance."

A silence descended as he regarded her with those
astonishingly beautiful blue eyes. Kate could almost
feel him weighing and calculating his response.

She had caught him off guard with her unexpected resistance. And perhaps forced him to alter
his angry response to her impertinent flight from

Kent. Now he carefully brooded upon how best to put her back beneath his heel.

"It appears that you are not inclined to be reasonable at the moment. Understandable, I suppose. You feel that I have treated you ill and are determined to punish me for my unwitting sins."

Her gaze narrowed in anger. Blast his arrogance. He thought that she was simply indulging in a fit of pique at being jilted. And that given a few charming apologies, she would readily forgive his betrayal. He had no notion of the depth of her frustration.

"If it pleases you to believe so."

His lips curved in a dangerous smile. "What would please me is if you would pack your bags and return to Kent."

Her chin tilted. "No. I intend to remain in London and fully enjoy my visit."

"Is that so . . . *Mrs. Freemont?*"

There was no mistaking the deliberate emphasis on her false name. Kate swallowed heavily. Bloody hell. He was warning her that he very firmly held the whip in his hand.

Her hands unconsciously curled into fists in her lap. "What do you want from me, my lord?"

He paused as his gaze deliberately trailed over her slender form. "I believe you know very well what I want. We have unfinished business in Kent."

Kate discovered the oddest shiver trickle down her spine at his intense survey. Almost as if she found his lingering gaze a source of forbidden excitement. Then, with stern determination, she forced herself to recall the painful humiliation he had delivered mere weeks ago.

"It is too late, Lord Calfield. I have decided that our . . . business is not what I desire after all."

He leaned even closer. Close enough for her to catch the scent of masculine cologne and warm male skin.

"I could force you to change your mind, you know. All I need do is send a message to Sir Frazer that you are not in Surrey as he so trustingly believes, and you would discover yourself hauled back to Kent in the blink of an eye."

Her fury threatened to boil over at the smooth threat. How dare he? How dare he toss her aside as if she were a worthless piece of rubbish and then smugly presume he could waltz back into her life as if nothing had occurred?

"You may be capable of forcing me back to Kent, but I assure you that it would only make me more determined than ever to avoid any relationship between us. Nothing could force me to speak with you again."

Checkmated by her fierce words, Calfield frowned in gathering annoyance. He was clearly torn between his arrogant desire to toss her over his shoulder and force her to his will and a budding suspicion that she might actually dare to defy him.

At last he gained command of his male impulses and turned to balefully study the gentleman sitting close to her side. Calfield's lean features appeared to harden at the sight of the other's sleek elegance and aggressive masculinity.

"Are you not going to introduce me to your . . . acquaintance?" he rasped.

"No," Kate retorted, thoroughly embarrassed at what Lord Thorpe must think of her. "I do not want you here. Not in this garden, not at this hotel, not in London. Go away."

Calfield turned back with a smile that did not

match his suddenly cold eyes. "And here I thought you would be pleased to see a friendly face."

"Your only thought was to bully me back to Kent. But I will not go. You might as well return to whatever it is that keeps you so occupied that you cannot recall which day it is."

"Oh no, I will not be leaving, my dear," he warned, sending a chill down her spine. "I intend to remain in London as long as necessary."

With a sudden motion, Lord Thorpe rose to his feet. "I hate to break up this . . . intriguing reunion, but I believe I should be returning to my home." The dark gaze warmly stroked over her flushed features. "Will you be attending the theater tonight?"

Vividly aware of Calfield's looming form, Kate gave a reckless smile. What woman with the least amount of sense would not leap at an opportunity to further her acquaintance with this gorgeous gentleman?

"Yes, I believe that I will."

"Lovely. Until then."

With a sweeping bow, Lord Thorpe turned to stroll back across the garden, leaving Kate alone with the man now regarding her with a simmering annoyance.

"I suppose he is the reason you are so reluctant to leave London? Have you decided he is a preferable choice to become your husband?" he grated.

Kate jumped to her feet and reached for her parasol. The lout was fortunate she did not swing it upside his head. While Lord Thorpe's admiring gaze had made her feel desirable, the manner in which Calfield kept inspecting her overly slender form was a potent reminder that she possessed none of the bumps and curves that made gentlemen's blood boil.

"For your information, I just met Lord Thorpe."

She roughly tugged at her spencer. "Although I do not comprehend why I am explaining anything to you. Who I may or may not marry is no longer your concern."

His hands landed on his hips, making the muscles beneath the clinging coat ripple with a fluid strength.

"You are still my fiancée."

"Fiancée? I have never been more to you than a tempting dowry." She gave a lift of her chin. "But no longer. Now I fear you must seek a new means of acquiring your fortune."

His brows drew together. "You were eager enough to wed me just a few weeks ago. Your feelings cannot have changed so swiftly."

"But they have. Everything has changed."

A sharp, disbelieving silence descended as he gave a slow shake of his head. "This is insanity, Kate," he burst out in obvious frustration.

"No, this is my life and I intend to enjoy it. Every moment of it. Pack your bags and go home, my lord. There is nothing you can say or do to change my mind."

She reached down to grab her reticule, and Calfield took a hurried step forward. "Where are you going?"

"Back to the hotel to change my attire," she informed in him crisp tones. "I am attending the most fascinating lecture on Egyptian mummies this afternoon."

Not giving him the opportunity to respond, Kate turned on her heel and marched toward the nearby hotel.

To hell with Lord Calfield, she told herself firmly.

If he wished to waste his time chasing after her, then so be it.

There was nothing he could do to force her into marriage. Not as long as she remained adamant in her refusal. Eventually he would tire of his game and leave.

Until then, she would carry on exactly as she had planned.

A hot bath.

An Egyptian lecture.

A brief nap.

And attending the theater with a man who was utterly breathtaking.

Yes, life was good.

Life was a royal pain in the backside.

Seated in the sinfully luxurious theater lobby, Luce stretched out his long legs and sipped his scotch.

He should have been on the docks.

There were always meetings to attend. Deadlines to meet. A payroll to sign.

A luscious mistress who would be delighted to return him to her bed.

Why the devil should he be chasing after a woman who obviously was not at all what he had thought? A woman who clearly possessed the temperament of a shrew and the tongue of a viper? A woman, moreover, who had made it clear that she considered him a worthless fortune hunter?

If he possessed the least scrap of sense, he would be rejoicing at having avoided an eternity with a woman destined to become a bitter, shrill spinster.

No, a silky voice whispered from the back of his mind. Never a spinster. Not with that firm and shockingly desirable form that had suddenly been revealed in the sheer crimson gown.

An unwelcome heat flooded his lower body as he recalled the sight of her attired as audaciously as any courtesan. For long moments, he had not even recognized his prim and proper fiancée.

Surely, Kate could not possess that delicate body that virtually begged for a man's touch? Or that heavy curtain of titian hair that had been left loose to shimmer with a seductive promise of hidden fires?

His body had reacted with a purely male instinct to her alluring attire. Not even the realization that it was indeed his fiancée could halt the stirring awareness.

And it had not helped to have that lusty Lord Thorpe panting beside her like a cur in heat.

He had wanted to sling Kate over his shoulder and carry her back to where she belonged. Or better yet, put his fist into the leering scoundrel's overly pretty face.

It was little wonder he had handled their encounter with the finesse of a fumbling buffoon, he wryly acknowledged. He had been caught off guard, startled by the undoubted transformation of Kate as well as her stubborn determination to court certain ruin.

Well, it would not be allowed to happen again.

He was prepared for anything.

Absolutely anything.

That rather smug thought had just passed through his mind when he lifted his head and Kate stepped into the lobby. With a startled gasp, he promptly choked on his scotch.

Bloody hell.

Although she had at least replaced the scandalous crimson gown in deference to the elegant surroundings, the daring jade gown she now wore was no more successful in covering her slender body. Barely skimming her shoulders, it hugged her slight bosom with a tenacious perfection, the skirts floating down in a river of silk. Beneath the candlelight, her skin glowed with a milky perfection and the sultry glow in her eyes added a potent sensuality that set fire to the very air.

His breath evaporated as she glided across the lush carpeting, her curls framing her pale countenance with a rich, vibrant temptation. A temptation shared by him and every other male in the room, if the stunned expressions were anything to go by, he acknowledged dryly.

So much for being prepared for anything.

Giving a shake of his head, Luce forced himself to his feet.

Very well, she was not the dowd she had pretended to be. In fact, there was absolutely nothing dowdy about her. Beneath those former ugly gowns and hideous caps, she had been a gentleman's deepest fantasy.

That did not alter the reason he had come to London. If anything, it made it all the more imperative that he whisk her back to Kent before some shallow rake managed to steal the heart that belonged solely to him.

"Good evening, Kate," he murmured, stepping directly into her path and forcing her to a halt. "What a pleasant surprise."

A brief flare of annoyance darkened her eyes to an interesting shade of green before she was determinedly offering him a tight smile.

"Hardly a surprise, I should think, my lord. You did after all know quite well that I would be here this evening."

He regarded her steadily. "I believe that I

requested you call me Luce when you accepted my proposal. It is not so difficult a name."

"But we are no longer engaged, Lord Calfield," she replied, deliberately using his formal title.

"By your choice, not mine."

She lifted her brows in a manner perfectly designed to set his teeth on edge. "I believe, sir, that you must have taken an unfortunate blow to the head. Or perhaps your advanced years have affected your memory. I was not the one who deliberately missed my own wedding. Indeed, I stood at the altar for nearly an hour awaiting your arrival. It was a most . . . enlightening experience."

Luce battled a sharp pang of guilt. Blast it all. He had not meant to hurt her. Perhaps he should have left London earlier. Or insisted that Foster take the ship out, and damn the storm. But . . .

But nothing, a small voice whispered in the back of his mind. He had behaved like an arrogant ass by treating his own marriage as if it were no more than an unwanted appointment that could be attended or missed at his convenience. Now, it was obvious he would have to pay for his indifference.

"I am sorry, you know," he said softly. "It was never my intention to hurt or humiliate you."

If he had hoped his words would melt her heart, he was to be sadly disappointed.

"It no longer matters. In truth, I should thank you for jilting me."

Luce did not like the sound of this. Not one little bit.

"Thank me?"

A genuine smile curved her lips. "Yes. Had you not left me at the altar, I would never have found the courage to come to London and truly seek my independence. You offered me something that I never expected to find."

"And what would that be?"

"Freedom."

He stilled. Dash it all. He had known he was not going to like her confession. And he most certainly did not.

She was not supposed to want her freedom. She was supposed to want marriage and security and children and social position. All the things he could offer.

Something in his chest squeezed in a most disconcerting manner.

"And . . . what do you intend to do with this freedom?"

A hint of enchanting color touched her cheeks. "That is really my business, is it not?"

"I am merely curious." He gave a faint shrug. "Do you devote every day to lectures on mummies?"

"Oh no, tomorrow I am invited to a tea to discuss Byron's latest poem and then a political dinner at Mrs. Roberts'. It should be quite fascinating."

Luce narrowed his gaze at the undisguised anticipation in her voice. "You really are enjoying yourself, are you not?"

"Yes, I am. Which is why it is pointless for you to remain."

Luce forced a smile, refusing to be goaded. Although he knew that he could force this woman into marriage by the simple means of calling for Sir Frazer, he was not willing to sink to such a desperate measure. At least not yet. He did not want her coming to him filled with anger and resentment.

He was fully confident that her burning embarrassment at being left at the altar would fade in time. And that she would realize that she was being a fool to turn her back on a marriage that would elevate her to the rank of a countess.

Until then, he intended to play his hand as any true gambler.

Calm, cool, and collected, he reminded himself.

"Now that I am here, I might as well enjoy a few days in London. My previous visits have usually entailed endless days upon the docks. It will be a pleasure to return to society."

Her lips thinned with annoyance. "You will not change my mind. I have no intention of wedding you."

"So be it."

"Lord Calfield . . ."

"It is Luce. And you have my word of honor that I will not attempt to bully you back to Kent," he interrupted, raising his hand in a solemn promise.

Kate regarded him with patent disbelief. "I do not trust you."

Luce could not prevent a rueful laugh. "That, I suppose, is our fundamental problem, is it not, my dear?"

Her expression remained decidedly wary. "You will not tell my father I am here?"

"No."

"And you will keep my true identity a secret?"

"If that is your desire."

"And no interfering in my life," she continued in warning tones.

"No interfering."

"If I wish to attend a boxing match, or visit a gambling hell, or wear daring gowns, you will not halt me."

Luce felt his heart come to a perfect halt as all sorts of delicious sensations whizzed through his body.

"Why would I desire to halt you?" he muttered,

his gaze dropping to the tempting expanse of white skin. "Although I would prefer that you reserve such gowns for my pleasure alone."

She sucked in a sharp breath, making him uncomfortably aware that little more than sheer will kept the dress in place.

"We will never be alone."

"Oh, we will be alone. Soon. And then I intend to tell you exactly how such a gown affects me," he said before he could halt the words.

"Luce."

"What?" Lifting his gaze, he met her stern frown with a wry smile. "Sorry, I was rather distracted."

A delicate color stained her cheeks. "I do not think a gentleman who deliberately left me at the altar should be regarding me in such a manner."

Was she daft?

He would have to be in his grave not to regard her in such a manner.

Only with an effort did he halt the urge to reach out and discover if that pale skin was as silky smooth as it promised.

"I did not deliberately leave you at the altar," he reminded her. "And soon enough you will be willing to listen to sense. Until then, I am just another gentleman dazzled by your beauty and anxious to win your regard."

She appeared momentarily taken aback by his insinuating words, then she abruptly stiffened, as if she were struck by a sudden thought.

"Oh, I see."

He lifted a golden brow. "What?"

"You cannot bully me into returning, so now you hope to seduce me back to Kent."

A far more pleasing prospect, he inwardly

acknowledged. The question was whether or not she would allow herself to be seduced.

"Am I succeeding?"

"No."

He gave a low laugh, stepping close enough to catch the aroma of her very feminine perfume. He inhaled deeply, realizing that the scent was uniquely Kate's. It had pervaded her home and at times clung to his coat long after he visited her. He knew he could close his eyes and sense when she was near. Odd that he had been so aware of such an intimate thing. Certainly, he would not recognize the scent of his mistress, or even his own mother.

"Then I shall simply have to increase my efforts," he promised in low tones.

Something flashed in her eyes as she took an awkward step backward. "Do not waste your time."

"It is my time to waste."

She regarded him warily, then with obvious relief, she spotted someone over his shoulder.

"Oh, Lord Thorpe has arrived."

Luce stiffened, turning to study the too handsome man in the too expensive gray coat and white pantaloons before returning his gaze to the woman at his side. He did not like her sudden smile of anticipation.

It made him want to hit something.

"What do you know of this Lord Thorpe?" he demanded abruptly.

She gave a faint frown at his preemptory tone. "Nothing beyond the fact that he possesses a town house in Mayfair."

"Do you really believe it is wise to indulge in a flirtation with a complete stranger?"

"What could possibly happen in a public theater?"

Luce gave a click of his tongue. Really, Kate

might have suddenly discovered she was a woman, but she clearly did not possess any more sense than a giddy schoolgirl.

"There are any number of alcoves and closets a gentleman can force a woman into—"

"No," she rudely interrupted, stabbing a finger directly in his face. "No interference."

"Kate . . ."

"You promised."

Luce's teeth snapped together with an audible click.

Damn. Damn. Damn.

He was trapped by his own ridiculous pledge.

"Fine." His features hardened in a dangerous manner. "But I will be keeping my eye on him. He is clearly a practiced rake. Indeed, his debauchery is obvious to anyone who would take the effort to study him closely."

She threw her hands up in disbelief. "You, my lord, are impossible."

Luce felt his jaw twitch with annoyance as she swept across the lobby to join Thorpe. It did not help matters that her brilliant smile as he leaned downward to whisper something in her ear could have lit the stage.

Luce may have promised not to interfere, but that did not mean he could not keep her under strict surveillance. From this moment on, she was not going to move a step without him firmly upon her heels.

CHAPTER THREE

Kate spotted him the moment she rounded the street to her hotel.

A tall, lean form that appeared disturbingly male in his buff breeches and moss green coat.

Leaning nonchalantly next to the door to the hotel, Luce simply waited for her to complete her stroll.

Not that she was surprised, she wryly acknowledged. Luce had become a tenacious barnacle that she could not easily dislodge.

Last evening, he had followed her into the theater where he had kept an unabashed surveillance upon her until she had at last left in annoyance. He had been in the garden when she sought a breath of fresh air. And even within the hotel when she had left for her tea.

It had been something of a surprise to discover he had not actually followed her to Mrs. Roberts' and thrust his unwelcome way into her home.

He was a dangerous impediment to her life of independence, she acknowledged as she closed the distance and felt his gaze sear over the sheer muslin gown that made no claim to modesty. Made even more dangerous by his obvious attempt to seduce her will.

Blast it all.

She was perfectly prepared to combat his arrogance and even his bullying tactics. She was not his property and she would not be treated as such.

But she was not so naive as to believe herself impervious to his masculine appeal. Since his arrival in London, she had been forced to admit that in some deep and basic manner she had been attracted to Luce from the moment her father had brought him into their home. Her skin tingled when he was near, her stomach knotted with pleasure when he accidentally brushed against her, and more than one night had been devoted to shameless dreams of her soon-to-be-husband.

Which was no doubt the reason his betrayal had hurt so dreadfully.

If he decided to try a full-on assault, she was not entirely certain she possessed the strength to deny him. That realization only made it all the more imperative that she convince him to leave, she sternly told herself.

Clearly her angry demands, even pleas, were falling on deaf ears. Her only hope appeared to be in remaining thoroughly indifferent to his presence. If she refused to react to his determined pursuit, he would eventually realize his cause was hopeless. And then he would be forced to seek a new means of acquiring his fortune.

With an effort, she forced a cheerful smile to her lips as she halted beside his tall form.

"Good afternoon, Luce."

"Kate." His own smile was far less easy to read. "How was the tea?"

"Lovely, thank you."

"I did not realize you were such a great admirer of Byron's."

She offered a faint shrug. "I enjoy a lively debate upon his merits."

"And you discovered such a debate at Mrs. Roberts'?"

"Actually, I did. Do you know there are gentlemen in London who are actually prepared to listen to a mere woman's view on literature?" She allowed her pleasure to glow in her eyes. "They are even prepared to accept that women might possess an actual ability to think for themselves. Can you imagine?"

He regarded her through half-lowered lids. "Quite easily. I have always known that you were an intelligent, well-educated woman. It was one of your most potent allures."

She sternly quenched the tiny thrill of pleasure at his low words. Her allure had been her dowry, nothing more.

"I find that difficult to believe."

"Why?"

She gave a lift of her shoulder. "We were hardly well enough acquainted for you to know if I possessed any intelligence or not."

"I assure you that having known any number of silly women, my sisters included, I do not need more than a few moments to distinguish a female of good sense." His smile deepened. "And besides, no maiden without a good deal of intelligence as well as perseverance could have managed to establish an orphanage that saved dozens of poor children from the brutal coal mines."

She floundered for a moment. To her knowledge, only Julia was fully aware of the effort she had put into seeing the orphanage built. She had taken great care to ensure that it was the vicar who received the bulk of the credit.

"How did you know?" she whispered.

"I made it my business to know, Kate," he murmured. "You are my fiancée. Everything about you fascinates me."

Fascinates? Oh, dash it all.

"I . . ." She determinedly sucked in a deep breath. "What are you doing here?"

His lips twitched. "That should be obvious, my dear. Where else would you have your devoted fiancé be?"

"Do I have a choice?" she demanded in overly sweet tones.

His low chuckle filled the air. "I suppose you would have me sent to the netherworld?"

"A tempting notion, although I would settle for Kent."

"As would I," he murmured. "As long as you were at my side."

"Enough." She folded her arms about her waist. She wanted to be away from Luce. He was too large. Too dominating. Too blasted handsome. "You have not yet told me what you are doing here."

He held up a slender hand. "Very well, my dear. I am here quite simply because this is where I am staying for the duration of my stay in London."

Her eyes widened in disbelief. No. Not even this gentleman was that audacious. Was he?

"You have chambers here? In this hotel?"

"Yes."

He was that audacious. "Drat it, Luce, you promised . . ."

"I am not interfering," he firmly cut into her angry words. "Unlike your charming Lord Thorpe, I do not possess a town house in Mayfair, or anywhere else. I must stay in some hotel and this one suits me as well as any other." He abruptly shrugged, his gaze running a restless path over her upturned face. "And speaking of Lord Thorpe, how was your evening with the aging roué?"

Her eyes widened. "Lord Thorpe is not an aging roué."

His nose flared at her ready defense of her new-found friend. Almost as if he were jealous of the gentleman. A ridiculous thought, although one she could not entirely dismiss.

"You may not recognize his species, but I assure you, I can do so with ease. I can also assure you that he has only one intention as far as you are concerned."

Kate shrugged. Although she had thoroughly enjoyed her evening with the handsome lord, it had been impossible to relax enough to invite a more intimate conversation. The knowledge that Luce was watching her every expression had made her stiff and uncomfortable.

Thankfully, her companion had easily sensed her mood and deliberately kept her entertained with lighthearted anecdotes of society.

A sensitive and thoughtful gentleman, she told herself. A gentleman far more worthy of her attention than Lord Calfield.

And yet, she had been unable to forget that cool blue gaze trained upon her with unnerving intensity.

"He is a perfectly polite and proper gentleman," she informed him with a tilt of her chin. "Unlike some others that I could name."

"Oh come, Kate, you are not that naive," he scoffed.

"What is that suppose to mean?"

"A handsome gentleman dangling after a supposedly lonely widow? It should be obvious to the most innocent female that he is the sort to prey upon the unwary."

Kate sucked in a furious breath at his condescending tone.

A serpent in her garden of paradise, indeed.

"Are you implying that I am somehow unworthy to inspire a gentleman's genuine regard? That every gentleman I encounter must only desire my body or my fortune?"

He frowned with a building irritation. "I merely meant that you have very little experience with gentlemen of his sort."

"Something I intend to correct if you would just leave me alone."

Her blunt words appeared to catch him off guard, and he gaped at her in disbelief before his features abruptly hardened.

"Even knowing what he is?"

"But I do not know what he is," she retorted in scathing tones. "And I am certainly not going to judge him upon the basis of your fevered imagination."

He glared at her for a long moment, no doubt struggling with the urge to shake her silly. Very few dared to oppose the Earl of Calfield's considerable will. Certainly not a mere woman.

"And if I am correct?" he gritted out.

She offered him a taunting smile. "Then he should have enough experience for the both of us."

With a cool dignity, she swept past him, refusing to give in to the childish desire to topple him from the steps or slam the door upon his arrogant nose.

The man was insufferable, she told herself.

To think he would imply that the only man she could interest would be a lust-filled debaucher who preyed upon the desperate and the lonely.

Her teeth clenched as she marched through the lobby of the hotel.

Very well, perhaps she was not destined to become the Toast of Society. Or to receive dozens of proposals.

But she was not such a fright as all that.

She was intelligent. Well-mannered. And capable of running the finest of households.

Not all gentlemen would consider her an easy means to a fortune or a meaningless night of pleasure.

Why the devil did he not return to Kent where he belonged?

Brooding upon her wounded pride, Kate stepped toward the nearby stairs.

Intent on fleeing to her room where she could gather her composure in peace, she failed to note the dark-haired gentleman leaning against the railing. It was not until he reached out and actually grasped her arm that she came to a startled halt.

"Mrs. Freemont." Lord Thorpe regarded her flushed features in a quizzical manner. "I hoped I would find you here."

"Oh." With a self-conscious smile, Kate pushed back a curl that had strayed from her tidy coiffure. "Good afternoon, my lord."

The dark gaze shifted over her shoulder to where Luce's form was still visible beside the window. "I see your acquaintance has decided to remain in London."

Kate's hands abruptly clenched at her side. "Unfortunately. I do not know why he does not return to Kent."

"No? Well, perhaps that is because you are not a man," Thorpe muttered in wry tones.

"What?"

"Nothing." Returning his gaze to her wide eyes, the gentleman offered her a smile that could melt stone. "I was hoping you would have dinner with me tonight."

"Tonight?" Absurdly, Kate found herself hesitating. Although she had no desire to give credence to Luce's ridiculous words, she knew deep inside she was not entirely certain of Lord Thorpe's intentions. A light flirtation was one thing. A full-out seduction was quite another. "I am not sure."

His head cocked to one side. "You do not wish to be with me?"

"We are still all but strangers," she hedged. "And I do not believe it would be entirely proper."

"Ah." He reached out to lightly brush the stray titian curl. "We can have dinner here if you prefer. There is nothing improper in a gentleman and widow sharing a meal in such a public place."

She studied the meltingly beautiful male features and determinedly squared her shoulders.

No.

She was not going to allow Luce to ruin this as well.

When she had come to London, it had been with the intention of indulging her desires. Every desire. Only a fool would toss aside the opportunity to become better acquainted with this delightful rogue.

"Very well," she agreed in firm tones.

"Good." He leaned forward to brush a light kiss over her forehead. "I will meet you at nine."

Kate watched his tall form disappear from the hotel. A prickle of awareness stabbed into her neck, assuring her that Luce had witnessed the entire scene through the window and that he was furious.

Good.

A smile curved her lips.

She hoped he was furious.

She hoped his head would explode.

* * *

Luce felt as if his head would explode.

Pacing his chambers, he kept one ear cocked for the sound of Kate returning from her dinner.

Damn that bloody Lord Thorpe.

How had he managed to rent a private dining room? Not only were the rooms typically booked weeks in advance, but the exorbitant cost put them well beyond the means of all but the most exclusive guests.

No doubt the scoundrel had used his influence and wealth like any treacherous rake.

Money and influence the poverty-stricken Lord of Calfield did not possess.

In any event, the lout's maneuver had ensured that he had managed to slip Kate from beneath Luce's very nose. And for nearly three hours, he had been left to stew in his growing frustration.

What was the damnable maiden thinking? Or not thinking.

She was an intelligent, sensible woman. Or at least she had been until she had seemingly plunged into this fit of madness.

Certainly, she was intelligent enough to realize it was sheer stupidity to place herself at the mercy of a strange man.

Anything could happen.

Anything.

Slamming a fist into his open palm, Luce spun on his heel and paced back across the room.

Fifteen minutes.

Fifteen more minutes and he was going in search of Kate.

Even if he had to tear apart every room in the hotel.

He paced to the window, to the armoire, and back to the door. Five minutes passed. Then another five. Then, just when he was debating which room to begin with, he at last heard the sound of footsteps in the hall. With long strides, he crossed the floor and wrenched open his door. Hurrying down the hall, he turned the corner into the side corridor. He was quick, but not quick enough, as he caught just a glimpse of Kate's slender form before she stepped into her room and the door swung shut.

For a moment, he halted in indecision. There had been no cry for help. No sound of struggle. She was seemingly well and locked in her chambers. The sensible choice would be to return to his bed and speak with Kate tomorrow.

Unfortunately, Luce was not in the mood to be sensible.

He wanted to assure himself that Kate was indeed unharmed. And perhaps just as importantly, he had to know if she was alone.

Refusing to dwell upon the wisdom of his decision, Luce moved to the door and raised his hand to knock. At the same moment, the sound of breaking glass resounded through the air. His heart nearly halted as he slammed his fist against the smooth wood.

"Kate," he called roughly. "Kate, open this door."

A nerve-racking moment passed before the door opened and Kate regarded him with a puzzled frown.

"Luce, what do you want?"

"I heard a crash." Without ceremony, he stepped past her slight form and into her room. A battalion of French could not have kept him out. "What occurred?"

"Oh." Allowing the door to close, Kate moved

toward a nearby table. With an oddly unsteady motion, she sank to her knees next to the shattered crystal vase that had fallen and spilled numerous blood red roses over the carpet. "I knocked over the lovely flowers that Lord Thorpe sent to me."

"Roses. Predictable," Luce muttered, casting a jaundiced glance around the small but tidy chamber. "Where is the lecher?"

Her head abruptly lifted to stab him with an unfocused glare. "Lord Thorpe is not a lecher. He is a perfectly respectable gentleman."

"A perfectly respectable gentleman who no doubt has made a practice of seducing and abandoning young ladies."

"If you are going to be unpleasant, my lord, then you may take yourself to your own chambers," she huffed, clenching her hand about the crystal shards in her hand without thinking. "Ow."

"Here, let me," Luce commanded in impatient tones, bending down beside her to take the sharp glass from her fingers.

Clearly caught off guard, Kate hastily attempted to retreat from his proximity. Her awkward motion, however, succeeded in nothing more than sending her sprawling backward on the carpet.

"Humph."

Dropping the glass, Luce regarded the ungainly form with a gathering frown.

Once again, she had managed to discover a gown that was a breath from indecent. A silver satin creation with a bodice that only made a token effort to cover the slender curves. Less than a token effort at the moment, as the skirts were deliciously tugged up to her knees, revealing slender legs and a disturbing glimpse of lacy stockings.

Desire as sharp as a rapier sliced though him before he rigidly gritted his teeth.

"Kate, are you foxed?" he accused in strained tones.

"Certainly not," she denied, then as his brows rose in disbelief, she gave a small shrug. "I am pleasantly giddy."

"You are pleasantly cast to the wind," Luce retorted, rising to his feet so he could scoop her from the paisley rug and carry her to the adjoining chamber complete with a wide bed. Concentrating his anger toward the letch that had obviously seduced Kate into indulging far too freely, he somehow managed to pretend the feel of her soft feminine form pressed against his body was not stirring to life things better left unstirred. He laid her upon the mattress, then perched on the edge of the bed, careful to keep his gaze upon her flushed face. "What the devil was that idiot thinking to allow you to get in this condition?"

"My condition has nothing to do with Lord Thorpe."

"Fah. I do not doubt that he did this on purpose. Gentlemen such as your precious Lord Thorpe will do whatever is necessary to take advantage of a woman. Thank God you had enough sense to send him on his way."

"But I did not."

Luce stilled at her stunning confession. "What?"

"I did not send him on his way. I asked him to escort me to my door." Sinking deeper into the pillows, Kate allowed her heavy lashes to lower to her cheeks. "He walked me to the stairs, but he would not come a step further. He said that he could not take advantage of me. I wonder if he was just lying to protect my pride?"

Luce flinched as if he had just been kicked in the stomach by a very large, very angry mule.

"You asked him to escort you to your door?"

"Mmm."

"Are you in love with him?" he demanded harshly.

She gave a small giggle, clearly unaware of what she was saying or doing.

"Of course not. Although he is very, very charming. And beautiful. And a perfect gentleman."

Luce studied the relaxed features, wondering where his timid, biddable bride had disappeared to. Despite his undoubted male approval of her transformation, he discovered that he missed the maiden who had stirred his heart with her sweet innocence.

"Kate, tell me why you are in London," he prompted softly.

"I wish to enjoy myself," she muttered. "And why should I not? Other ladies do."

"You are not other ladies. You are an innocent maiden who should be in the care of your father. Or preferably, your husband. This foolishness might very well destroy your future."

"What future? Married to a gentleman who desires me only for my wealth? Or better yet, the dutiful daughter growing into a bitter old spinster? Quite something to envy, is it not?"

He frowned at her sharp tone. "Is that what you believe?"

"What else could I believe?" she demanded. "For four and twenty years I have been tedious, starchy Miss Frazer. The woman who always followed the rules of others, who never took a risk, who never had an adventure in her entire dull life. Well, no more. I am going to do all the things I have ever wanted to do."

"And what is it you want to do?"

"I am going to be just like my mother. Well, perhaps not precisely like her," she amended. "But at least I intend to do more than watch the mold grow in the country."

"Your mother?" Luce frowned at the absurd words. "What the devil does that mean?"

"You know . . ." She lowered her voice to a husky whisper. "The Jezebel."

"Jezebel?"

"That is what Father calls her. You see, she ran off with a handsome Frenchman. A terrible scandal, of course, although no one is allowed to discuss it. And I have her blood. Bad blood. Wicked blood that must not be tempted. Oh no. No temptation for Miss Frazer."

Luce's heart came to a halt. He had heard the old gossip. But somehow he had not fully realized how such an ancient scandal would have affected Kate. Certainly, he could never have suspected that she would believe that she possessed the weaknesses of her mother.

"That is absurd, my dear. Whatever the sins of your mother, you are innocent."

"My father does not believe so," she said sadly.

"Oh, Kate," he breathed in soft tones.

"But, now he is not here to condemn me." With an effort, she forced open her eyes. "Now I can live my life precisely as I desire."

His heart squeezed at her slurred words.

So now he had the reason for Kate's sudden insanity.

Damn Sir Frazer. And damn himself. Together they had managed to drive Kate to this madness.

"And that is why you wished to leave Kent?"

"Yes." She gave a slow nod of her head. "I do not want to be boring, tedious Miss Frazer anymore. I do not want to sit in the corner while everyone else is allowed to seek their enjoyment."

He smiled wryly. "Such as teas and the theater?"

"Mmm . . . and riding through Hyde Park and wearing daring gowns."

He absently reached out to stroke a finger over her hand. How frustrated she must have been, he thought with a pang. It was no wonder she was going a little insane.

Thank goodness he had followed her. There was no telling how far she might go before her senses returned.

"Of course," he murmured. "Is there anything else on that list of desires?"

"I want to see the Prince and dance the waltz."

"Very ambitious."

She smiled with a fuzzy pleasure. "Oh, and I want to eat escargots and have a glorious flirtation with a handsome gentleman."

Luce's indulgent expression was wiped away by the offhand words.

Riding in the park or meeting the Prince was one thing. He could even tolerate the offensive thought of escargots. But to encourage the attentions of some lust-crazed male? Oh no, that was an entirely different matter.

"A flirtation?"

Clearly missing the dangerous edge in his voice, Kate heaved a regretful sigh.

"It certainly seems more appealing than becoming a sour old spinster who has never been kissed."

His teeth gritted. His hands clenched. And his heart forgot to beat.

"That was why you asked Thorpe to escort you to your room?"

"Of course." She heaved a sorrowful sigh. "I thought if he had me alone he would kiss me."

Luce sucked in a sharp breath. The mere thought of Lord Thorpe kissing those lips, perhaps running his hands over that slender body, was enough to make him think of murder. He would see Thorpe, or any other rogue for that matter, in hell first.

"No," he growled in low tones.

She gave a vague frown. "No, what?"

"He would not have kissed you."

"Fah. How could you possibly know?"

With a deliberate motion, Luce shifted until he was leaning over her slight form, his hands planted on each side of her head.

"Because I would have killed him first."

She sank into the pillows, her eyes wide as she belatedly sensed the sudden tension in the air.

"You have nothing to do with this. No interference, remember? If I want to have a flirtation . . ."

"You will do so with me," he announced in tones that would not be gainsaid.

"What?"

He smiled wryly, not surprised by her stunned expression. He wasn't sure himself where the words had come from.

He had come to London with every intention of collecting Kate and hauling her back to Kent. He was not about to allow her to avoid for another moment the vows she had promised to make.

Certainly, he had never imagined allowing her to linger in this hotel risking certain scandal as she made him dance to her tune.

Now, he discovered himself hesitating.

Would it be such a horrid thing to spend a few

days indulging her wishes? Whatever her protest, in the end they would be wed. Would it not be preferable to have her come to him as an eager bride?

If she desired a bit of adventure, he was more than capable of providing all the excitement she desired.

And in the process, he could ensure that she realized that he was nothing at all like her bully of a father.

"I think you heard me, Kate," he said in husky tones.

"I cannot have a flirtation with you."

His gaze dropped to her mouth, unwittingly judging the satin softness. He discovered he very much wanted to kiss her. No, to savor her, he inanely corrected himself, like a fine wine.

"Why not?"

"I . . . you want to marry me."

He could not prevent his sudden laugh. "Is that such a terrible thing?"

"Yes."

"Why?"

"You only want my money."

"You are wrong, you know," he murmured softly. "You are a beautiful, enticing woman, my dear. There is no gentleman who would not wish to enjoy a flirtation with you. No gentleman who would not long to possess you."

"Luce?" she breathed unsteadily.

He smiled deep into her bemused eyes. "If you are concerned that I do not possess the romantic skills of your rake, let me assure you that while my experience may not be as vast as his, my wish to please you is far greater."

Her breath seemed oddly elusive. "But, you do not desire to kiss me."

Not desire to kiss her? Heaven have mercy. Now he knew she was mad.

Against his better judgment, his gaze swept over her reclined form. With her hair spilling like satin fire over the crisp white pillows and her eyes darkened with emotion, she appeared as delectable as the most experienced temptress.

"That is perhaps the most ridiculous thing I have ever heard," he rasped, his heart jolting against his chest. "I have ached to kiss you since the moment I arrived in London."

"You are merely saying that to confuse me."

Luce growled deep in his throat, slowly lowering his head toward the temptation of her lips.

Obviously, she needed proof of his sincerity.

Well, never let it be said that he failed to satisfy a lady.

Especially a lady he fully intended to have as his own.

"Shall I show you just how wrong you are, my sweet Kate?"

CHAPTER FOUR

Kate thought she must be dreaming.

Lost in a golden haze of champagne, she watched as Luce slowly lowered his head and stroked his lips softly over her own. The caress was as soft as a whisper and yet Kate felt a bolt of lightening strike from her mouth to the pit of her stomach.

The startling heat made her heart lurch in abrupt shock.

She had always wondered what it would be like to be kissed by Luce, she acknowledged dreamily. She had even caught herself staring at those carved lips with a secret sense of excitement.

And now she did know.

A sharp, poignant pleasure filled her as she instinctively parted her lips. He readily accepted her silent invitation and deepened the kiss.

She could taste the scotch on his lips and smell the warmth of his skin. She felt the rasp of his beard upon her chin.

The combination was far more intoxicating than the expensive champagne that flowed through her blood. With a sigh of pleasure, she lifted her arms to wrap them about his neck.

"Bloody hell," Luce moaned, lifting himself away to regard her with a smoldering gaze.

Stunned by his sudden retreat, she regarded him with bewildered eyes. "What is the matter?"

Seated on the edge of the bed, he ran a not quite steady hand through his tousled hair.

"Kate, forgive me."

"Why did you halt kissing me?"

He grimaced, his jaw clenched as if he were in pain. "Because you are in no condition to do so."

Kate flinched as if she had been slapped. First Lord Thorpe and now Luce, she acknowledged with a savage pain.

What was it about her? Was she that undesirable? That lacking in charm?

Perhaps her only worth *was* her dowry.

"Not again," she muttered. "Why do you not just admit the truth? That you find my kisses repulsive."

His lean fingers abruptly captured her chin and sharply turned her back to meet his fierce expression.

"Do not be a fool," he rasped. "I would barter my own soul right now to continue kissing you. But your wits are clouded by champagne. If I truly thought you knew what you were doing we would not be having this conversation. We would not be having any conversation." His gaze flared over her slender body before returning to her pale face. "We would be standing before a vicar so that I could make you my own."

Feeling suddenly tired and confused by the odd sensations trembling through her, Kate closed her eyes.

"Please, just go away."

There was a long pause before she felt her hair being gently brushed from her forehead.

"Will you be all right?"

"What do you care?" she muttered.

"Yes, what do I care?" he said in oddly wry tones. "Pleasant dreams, Kate."

Kate was nearly asleep before he ever reached the door.

She just wanted to forget the wretched night.

Luce would never forget that most enticing night.

Who would have thought that prim and proper Miss Kate Frazer, his soon-to-be-bride, could bemuse him with such ease?

Certainly, he had already acknowledged that she was a pretty enough woman. And that she was the sort of intelligent, well-bred maiden that a gentleman in his position could claim with pride.

But he had been unprepared for the sweet tenderness that had raced through his heart. His lips had touched hers, and all thoughts of dowries, overbearing fathers, and endless debts had been shattered.

There had been only Kate and the warmth that she offered.

A warmth that he had never even realized was missing from his life.

Pacing the garden, Luce allowed a small smile to curve his lips. Ah yes, she would make a delightful wife.

Kindly toward his tenants, devoted to her family, intelligent enough to provide endless evenings of lively conversation, and spirited enough to ensure he was never bored.

If he had devoted an entire lifetime to choosing the perfect bride, he could not have done better.

Now all he needed to do was convince her that he would make an equally fine husband.

Unfortunately, it was a task that might not be nearly as simple as he had once supposed.

His smile somewhat faded as he recalled her unwitting confessions of the night before. He had presumed her flight from Kent was no more than a maidenly bout of annoyance. He had, after all, treated her abominably. She had been embarrassed before the entire neighborhood and she intended to ensure that he was suitably punished.

All he needed to do was to offer a grudging apology and they would be headed down the aisle, he had thought.

He could not have realized that her abrupt disappearance was a desperate bolt for freedom. Nor that she would possess an unrelenting need to taste of the pleasures so long denied her.

A rather ironic dilemma, he wryly acknowledged.

When he had agreed to marry Kate, his only thought had been upon his own loss of independence. He understood his duty, but it still had seemed a wrenching sacrifice, to be made for the sake of his family. It had not occurred to him that Kate might possess her own share of reluctance.

Somehow gentlemen throughout England were under the misapprehension that all females were eager, if not downright desperate, to wed. And if the woman was so very fortunate as to capture a proposal from a titled gentleman, well then, she should be swooning with pleasure.

It was rather a shock to encounter a maiden who not only did not wish to become his wife, but in some vague manner, even feared the possibility.

Ironic, indeed.

Absently, Luce glanced up at the window of Kate's chambers and heaved an impatient sigh. He had expected her in the garden hours ago. She was, it seemed, irresistibly drawn to the serene beauty. At the very least, he thought he might see her bustling from the hotel on her way to some damnable lecture or tea.

It was utterly unlike her to remain in her chambers so late.

Was she still abed? Perhaps too ill to arise?

It would hardly be surprising. She had, after all, been shockingly foxed. For a woman unaccustomed to such indulgence, she might very well be suffering from a thick head.

Or worse.

He wavered briefly. It was the thought of that "or worse" that abruptly hardened his features and put his feet into motion. The stubborn woman had not even possessed the sense to bring a maid on her hasty flight to London. Who would know if she were in need of assistance?

Entering the hotel, Luce halted in the public rooms long enough to demand a tray loaded with steaming black coffee and a small platter of buttered toast before sweeping back up the stairs. He ignored the raised brows of the various guests as he carried his burden carefully down the hall. What did he care if others considered that carrying a tray like a common minion was beneath him? He had never given a damn what others thought of him. A gentleman willing to enter the rather disreputable trade of shipping could not afford to worry over trivial gossip.

It was not until he actually reached Kate's door that he realized his dilemma. Glancing at the precarious coffee perched on the tray, he gave a sudden grimace. Damn and blast. How the devil did maids manage? Surely they did not possess an extra arm that they kept tucked out of sight?

Unable to conjure a means of performing his task with any grace, Luce at last raised his foot and kicked the door by way of a knock. There was a long silence before he could at last hear the sound of the handle turning, and the door was slowly cracked open. He did not await an invitation or even the opportunity for Kate to realize what was occurring. Pressing his shoulder against the wooden panel, he pushed his way through the opening, his lips twitching as Kate scuttled backward with a small squeak of surprise.

"Luce, what the devil are you doing?"

He regarded her rumpled appearance with a stab of sympathy. She was still attired in the wrinkled silver gown of the night before, her hair in tangles and her face tinged with an unpleasant hint of green. Thankfully, she did not appear to be suffering from anything more serious than a wretched hangover.

"Good morning, my dear," he murmured, walking to place the tray upon a low table next to the window. Then, sweeping open the curtains, he turned to regard her with a smile. "It is a beautiful day."

With a tragic moan at the sudden spill of light into the shadowed sitting room, she regarded him with a jaundiced expression.

"Beast," she croaked.

He chuckled as he placed his hands on his hips. "Lovely to see you, as well. Are you ready for breakfast?"

She shuddered at the mere mention of food. "No. I feel wretched."

Luce allowed his gaze to travel over her rumpled form. "You look even worse."

"Oh . . ." She began, only to raise a shaking hand to her lips. "I am going to be sick."

Having already predicted the natural conclusion to her night of revelry, Luce was swift to pluck her into his arms and carry her to the adjoining chamber.

"I feared I might find you in this condition," he murmured as he carried her past the bed and toward the muslin screen in a far corner.

"Put me down," she demanded in weak tones.

"In a moment." Moving behind the screen he bent to gently place her on the floor beside the chamber pot. "You might as well make yourself comfortable. You are going to be here for some time." He met her gaze with a wry smile. "Call me if you need me, I will be just outside."

He softly crossed back into the sitting room as she moaned, although he left the door open to hear if she called out. It might have been years since he had become deliberately foxed, but the memory of the morning after lingered with vivid regret.

Absently strolling toward the table that held the breakfast tray, Luce poured himself a cup of the steaming coffee and glanced out the window.

He discovered himself smiling, although there was no possible excuse for the peculiar contentment that was settled within him. Good gads, he should be furious. Not only at having to tend to his reluctant bride, who had audaciously been out drinking with a common rake. But at the knowledge she had risked certain scandal, and her own innocence, by her ridiculous behavior.

But anger was not what he felt.

He felt . . . what?

Like a husband, a soft voice whispered in the back of his mind.

Surely this was what it was to be a husband? To concern himself with Kate's welfare. To know that it was his efforts that would bring her comfort.

To be at her side when she was in need.

Sharp, male possession surged through him. For the moment, her rattled wits might deny she belonged to him, but he knew the truth. He knew it with a deep, unshakable certainty.

She belonged to him.

Lock, stock, and barrel.

Breathing in the air that was filled with her sweet scent, Luce heard the footsteps behind him. Turning, he watched as Kate shuffled toward the narrow sofa and sank onto the edge.

"I think I must have caught the plague," she muttered.

He gave a low laugh. "No, not the plague. Just the usual punishment for too much champagne."

"I do not suppose I will be fortunate enough to die soon?" she demanded, looking like a battered flower with her hair tangled about her white face.

"No, I fear you will survive," he assured her with a faint smile. "Thankfully, by this afternoon you should be feeling considerably better." He reached to pour her a cup of coffee. "Drink this and try to eat something. As difficult as it might be to believe, it will help settle your stomach."

She shuddered but obediently reached for the coffee, which she sipped with a good measure of caution.

"Dear heavens. I never realized how ghastly I would feel."

"Like every pleasure in life, champagne has its cost," he said, suppressing his amusement at the sight of her misery. There was little of the demure, always proper Miss Frazer about her this morning, but he discovered it oddly moving to see her so vulnerable. "You did not believe that your lovely adventures could be had without a price, did you?"

She managed a glare, her eyes more blue than green this morning. "Could you please save your lectures, Luce? I am in no humor this morning."

He laughed as he reached for the plate of warm buttered toast. "Then eat."

She grimaced and leaned back in distaste. "No, I thank you."

"Having considerably more experience in your current condition, allow me to be the expert," he commanded, pressing a slice of toast into her unwilling fingers. "Eat."

Too ill to argue properly, she reluctantly nibbled at the edge of the toast. Eventually deciding it was not going to make her nauseated again, she reached for another slice.

Within several minutes, the tinge of green had left her features and Luce gave a nod of satisfaction.

"Is that better?"

"I suspect that I might live," she conceded, working her way through her third slice. "The world has stopped spinning and my stomach is not threatening an immediate revolt. I . . . what happened last night?"

Luce raised a golden brow at her hesitant question. "You do not recall?"

A vague frown marred her forehead as she struggled to battle through her foggy memories.

"I recall having dinner with Lord Thorpe and coming up to the room. And then you came to the door . . . and there were roses on the floor and . . ." She frowned with impatience. "After that I can recall nothing."

Luce froze. There was no denying the sharp blow

to his pride. Blast it all. He had lain awake for hours battling the lingering effects of her sweet, tempting kiss. Even his dreams had been plagued with the pleasures that awaited him in the marriage bed. And for her it was a moment lost in the cloud of champagne.

Still, he had to acknowledge that her lack of memory might be for the best. She had revealed the most intimate contents of her heart last night. It was quite possible that she would fiercely regret her confessions. And resent him for possessing her secrets.

Perhaps it would be best to keep the truth of last evening to himself.

Well, at least most of last evening, he corrected with a wicked smile. There were some parts he definitely intended her to recall.

"I must say that I am deeply wounded, my love. For me it was a night that shall be forever branded upon my memory," Luce devilishly murmured.

She stiffened in a wary manner. "What do you mean?"

He moved to settle himself on the sofa close beside her, laying his arm along the back of the cushions so that his fingers could lightly brush her shoulder.

"Well, it was our first kiss. A most momentous moment, or so most maidens seem to feel. Still, I suppose there will be endless more kisses for you to hold as keepsakes."

Her eyes widened in dismay. "You . . . kissed me?"

Gads, she made it sound as if he had tumbled her into the bed and ravished her, he acknowledged wryly. Well, two could play at that game.

"I did, but only after you so prettily begged me to do so."

A palpable shock filled the air. "I did no such thing."

"Shall I tell you the precise words that you used?" he murmured softly. "Or perhaps you would prefer that I tell you of how your arms wrapped about my neck and your lips . . ."

"You are merely roasting me," she at last managed to choke.

His hand moved upward and brushed a titian curl. He discovered his fingers lingering at the silken texture. Fire and silk; it was a fascinating combination.

Of course, he was learning that every stubborn, mysterious part of Miss Frazer held a certain fascination. In Kent she had been demure and sweetly innocent. Last night she had been bold and reckless. This morning she was vulnerable and uncertain.

His lips curled with a wry smile. It would take him a lifetime to discover all the hidden depths of this maiden. And much to his surprise, he realized that he was looking forward to the journey.

"There is no need to appear so shocked, my love," he assured her. "I was more than pleased to oblige your request. Indeed, I eagerly place myself at your disposal whenever the urge might come upon you again."

Her eyes darkened, as if vaguely sensing that something had indeed occurred during her bout of madness, and with a jerky motion, she set aside her empty cup.

"That will not be necessary," she retorted in a tight voice. "Last evening I was . . . I was not at all myself."

"Ah, but you assured me that you were only pleasantly giddy."

"Obviously, I was a great deal more than giddy. I

would never have allowed you through the door, let alone requested that you . . . you . . . kiss me, if I had not been out of my wits."

He lifted his brows at her less than flattering declaration. If it were not for the fact he knew damn well that she had eagerly responded to his touch, he might have been angered by her refusal to acknowledge the undoubted attraction between them.

As it was, he merely smiled. "Then I must make a note to order several crates of champagne for our wedding breakfast, my love. I shall definitely desire you to allow me through the door on our marriage night."

A flustered blush added a much-needed color to her white countenance as she tilted her chin to a combative angle.

"You may order all the champagne that you desire, but I assure you that there is not going to be a wedding," she retorted. "Not ever."

His smile dimmed as he regarded her stubborn expression. Gads. He had promised her a flirtation. Even if she did not recall the promise. But how the devil was he to woo her when she was determined to treat him with such distrust?

"Are you always so unforgiving, Kate?" he asked softly, claiming her gaze with his own. "I have attempted to apologize for my boorish behavior and to seek some means of healing the wounds that you suffered. What must I do to earn your pardon?"

She appeared unbalanced by his direct attack. "I . . . it is not a matter of forgiveness."

"No?" He tilted his head to the side. "Then you are not attempting to punish me?"

"I have told you that I have put the past behind me."

"If that is true, why do you insist that we will never

wed?" he demanded in low tones. "Unless there is some other reason you have so adamantly decided we should not suit?"

Her tongue peeked out to wet her lips, and Luce briefly worried that she would flatly refuse to answer. Then, clasping her hands in her lap, she drew in a steadying breath.

"I have decided that I prefer not to be wed for my wealth."

Well. That was as straightforward as a shovel to the head. He gave an uncomfortable cough.

"I see." He took a moment to carefully choose his words. Kate was too intelligent to believe any vague prevarications. Nor would she be easily swayed with sweet words and empty flattery. It appeared his only choice was the truth. "You believe my only interest is in your dowry?"

She regarded him steadily. "Can you deny that my father offered you a sizable fortune to take me as a wife?"

"He did approach me with such a proposition," he conceded. "Sir Frazer was aware of my own father's charming habit of tossing away his fortune at the gaming tables and believed that I would be anxious to acquire the funds necessary to keep my estate from tumbling into ruin." He paused, not missing the manner in which her jaw tightened. "I refused."

Her eyes abruptly narrowed in blatant disbelief. "Balderdash."

Luce gave a lift of his shoulder. "It is the truth, Kate. I had no intention of being purchased like a horse upon a block simply because your father desired my bloodlines."

She did not appear the least impressed with his

explanation. Indeed, she seemed more offended than ever.

"If you did not wish to wed me, then why, pray tell, did you ever propose?"

"Because I met you," he said simply.

"What?"

"After I refused your father's proposal, he insisted that I join him for dinner to assure there were no hard feelings between the two of us." Luce could not prevent his lips from twitching with wry amusement. "As you must know, your father can be rather . . . insistent when he chooses."

She could not halt her revealing grimace. "Yes."

"He was a wise gentleman. He must have known that I expected a tediously dull evening enduring a full-out assault by a desperate, brazen woman who was on the hunt for a title." Luce's gaze shifted to the titian curl that he had wrapped about his finger. "Instead, I was greeted by a shy, astonishingly gentle maiden. A maiden who seemed quite capable of offering her heart to an awkward earl who feels more comfortable among the docks than among the *ton* and a fluttering collection of female relatives who would be bound to smother her with their attentions. To be frank, you appeared eminently suitable to claim the title of Countess of Calfield."

"I . . ." She gave a slow shake of her head, as if not yet prepared to accept the truth of his words. "You could not possibly have known anything about me. You rarely bothered to call and when you did so, it was only in passing."

Luce gave a nod of his head, fully aware that he deserved her criticism.

"You have the right to be disappointed in me, Kate. I was shamefully inattentive as your fiancé." He heaved a rueful sigh. "It would be a simple matter to blame my neglect upon the burdens of my business, or even the duties of learning to be an earl. It was what I told myself. But in truth, I fear I was merely uncomfortable and not at all certain what to do with you."

She blinked in confusion. "What to do with me?"

Luce's lips twisted in self-derision. "Unlike most gentlemen, I have never spent much time among society. My only experience has been among females who make no demands upon a gentleman and possess few expectations. Certainly, I have never learned the delicate art of wooing an innocent maiden. I feared I might make an utter ass of myself if I tried to win your affection." He gave a short, humorless laugh. "Instead, I managed to wound your feelings and, in the end, to lose you entirely."

She faltered at his stark revelations, as if being forced to consider him as more than the arrogant, cold-hearted beast she had convinced herself he must be.

Still, her eyes remained guarded as she met his piercing gaze. "That does not alter the fact that you would not be marrying me if it were not for my fortune."

Luce abruptly shifted so that he could lay his hands upon her shoulders. There would be no more misunderstandings between them. He knew from experience that they could only move forward if the past was laid to rest.

"Just as you would not wed a gentleman unless he were of proper birth and social position," he said firmly. "It is your duty to your family to offer them connections that would otherwise be above them, just as my duty is to ensure the welfare of my family. That does not mean that we cannot come to care for one another or to find happiness in our marriage."

"No." She jerkily raised her hands to press them to her temples. "Please, Luce. I do not wish to discuss this now. My head is still aching and I cannot think clearly."

His lips thinned with impatience but he reluctantly forced himself to remove his hands from her shoulders. The most certain way to lose her was to attempt to force her to his will.

It was, after all, what her father would do.

"As you wish." He offered her a smile. "Why do you not ring for a hot bath, and once you are feeling more the thing, you can join me downstairs?"

"Why?" she demanded warily.

"I thought we might spend a few hours enjoying some of the sights." He grimaced at the shadows beneath her eyes. "I doubt your constitution will be up for more strenuous pleasures until tomorrow."

"I am to join Lord Thorpe for a ride in the park later this afternoon," she said in defiant tones.

Luce's features briefly tightened before he forced himself to relax.

"Very well," he conceded with an unconsciously predatory smile. "But you are having dinner with me."

"Luce."

He abruptly rose to his feet, realizing he had to get out of the room.

One more mention of Lord Thorpe and he would resort to his original plan to toss her over his shoulder and head for the nearest vicar.

"Do not linger too long in your bath, Kate," he commanded in dark tones. "I shall be awaiting you in the garden."

Without giving her the opportunity to protest, Luce turned about and left the room. He moved down the hall with long strides and shoved open the door to his own chambers.

At his entrance, Foster pushed himself from the chair where he had been impatiently awaiting Luce's arrival.

"It's about bloody time," the old sailor muttered in sour tones. "I have been waiting here for near an hour."

Luce shrugged, crossing the room to pour a large measure of brandy. With one motion, he drained the fiery spirits down his throat.

"I fear there has been a change of plans, Foster," he said, turning to regard his companion. "I will not be joining you at the docks this morning."

Foster folded his arms over his barrel chest. "Chasing after that woman, I suppose."

Luce smiled grimly at the hint of disapproval in the gruff voice. "Must I remind you that that woman is soon to be the next Countess of Calfield?"

"And must I remind you that you wouldn't be chasing after her like a hound on the scent if you hadn't been late to your wedding as I warned?"

"I am painfully aware of my folly, thank you, Foster," he retorted in wry tones. "Now I must do what I can to repair the damage. And for that I need your assistance."

The hardened sailor recoiled in horror. "My assistance? With a proper lady?"

Luce lifted a slender hand. "Be at ease, you cowardly dog. I know you are allergic to the fairer sex. Or at least to those who do not frequent the taverns. What I need from you is information."

"What sort of information?"

Luce narrowed his gaze. "Whatever you can discover on a Lord Thorpe. Especially any scandals that might be attached to his name, and if he is in need of a fortune."

The bushy brows rose in surprise at his clipped command. "Competition, Luce?"

"The enemy, Foster." A hard smile touched his lips. "One I intend to defeat before he ever reaches the battlefield."

CHAPTER FIVE

"It is . . . magnificent," Kate murmured in wonder, leaning over the metal railing in the Whispering Gallery of St. Paul's Cathedral toward the patterned marble floor below. "What does the book say?"

Luce appeared remarkably content for a gentleman who had devoted the past two hours to trailing behind her as she wandered through the beautiful church. He obediently leafed through the small pamphlet he had purchased before beginning the tour.

"Let me see, the fresco paintings within the dome were the work of James Thornhill, and that railing you are currently leaning against was created by Jean Tijou. Below us you will find an epitaph for Wren carved into the floor. It is written in Latin, but it translates to: 'Beneath lies buried the founder of this church and city, Christopher Wren, who lived more than ninety years not for himself but for the public good. Reader, if you seek his monument, look around you.'" He lifted his amused gaze to meet her expectant expression. "More?"

"Of course. You cannot properly appreciate such beauty without knowing the history, can you?"

"After eight and twenty years of presuming that it was perfectly possible, it appears I labored under a dire misapprehension. I do thank you for correcting my tasteless lack of sensibility," he teased with that gentle humor that continued to catch Kate off guard.

Of course, if she were perfectly honest with herself, there were a great number of things about Luce that had caught her off guard since his arrival in London.

Her heart gave an odd squeeze as she recalled his arrival in her chambers that morning. Gads, surely almost any gentleman would have fled in horror when she embarrassed herself by nearly sicking up all over him? Instead, Luce had competently taken charge and even managed to make her feel better when she had been certain she was hovering near death.

And then he had sat beside her and so earnestly attempted to convince her that he did not consider her a mere source of ready wealth. That he believed she was perfectly suited to be his bride and Countess of Calfield. And that he had been as uncertain and anxious as herself . . .

With a considerable effort, Kate thrust the memories aside. No. She had determined when she so reluctantly left her chambers this morning that she would not dwell upon her sudden bout of uncertainty.

Whatever confessions Luce might have offered changed nothing, she assured herself firmly. She had come to London with a purpose and nothing he might say or do would alter her determination.

Feeling his gaze resting upon her expressive countenance, she forced a calm smile to her lips. She was the new, daring Miss Kate Frazer, she reminded herself sternly.

"Wren was obviously a genius," she murmured.

There was a glint in the blue eyes that warned he suspected at least a portion of her inner unease, but thankfully he did attempt to press her.

"Obviously, and like most geniuses he was also a bit batty. It says here that when this dome was being completed, he had himself hauled up in a basket two or three times a week to ensure all was going to his plan." He glanced the long distance down to the smooth marble below. "Can you imagine swinging about in a basket when you are seventy-six years of age?"

Her nose wrinkled. "I cannot imagine swinging in a basket at any age."

He leaned his large frame against the railing, studying her beneath half-lowered lids. "Not even for the sake of such a glorious work of art?"

She glanced about the ornate perfection that glowed like a jewel. A sense of awed peace filled her heart as she breathed deeply of the hushed air.

"You are right. I believe I would have dangled in a basket from sunup to sundown if I could have created something so wonderful," she admitted with a wistful smile. "How splendid it must be to watch a dream taking form stone by stone, brushstroke by brushstroke."

"Yes, there is nothing so satisfying as shaping something from nothing."

She regarded him with a searching gaze, intrigued by his low words.

"You speak of your shipping company?"

He blinked as if startled that she had sensed his deeper meaning.

"Yes, I suppose I do." He smiled with a boyish charm. "Although a handful of ships can hardly compare to a work of such wonder."

"I would not think that it is the size or the

grandeur of the dream that is important, but the dream itself," she murmured as her hands skimmed over the smooth railing. She was startled by the odd ache that clutched at her heart. Determinedly, she sucked in a deep breath. "Tell me, how did you ever come to own a shipping company?"

He searched her guarded expression for a moment before offering a faint shrug.

"It was actually more a fluke than choice. Ten years ago, I happened to win a ship in a card game, although it was rather a jest to claim the pile of rotting timbers as anything beyond a ruin. In truth, I had every intention of selling it to the first gullible fool who would give me a quid when I happened to go down to the docks and stepped onto the deck." His lean features unwittingly softened with a deep sense of pride. "In that moment, I realized that I could do more with my existence than waltz through ballrooms or follow my father's footsteps into the gambling hells."

"You enjoy your business?"

His lips twitched at her hint of surprise. "I enjoy the challenge. Even the risk. I hazard the entire future of my company with every cargo I purchase. It is a gamble each and every day."

The unmistakable glitter of pleasure that warmed his blue eyes summoned that ridiculous ache once again. Her fingers tightened upon the rail as she considered the source of her discomfort.

"I must say that I envy you," she admitted slowly, her brow unconsciously wrinkled as she sorted through her strange emotions. "I cannot recall ever possessing a dream that I could follow."

Thankfully, he did not treat her confession with an offhand dismissal. Instead, his expression became somber as he reached out to gently brush a curl that lay against her cheek.

"Surely you must have harbored dreams as a young girl?"

She gave a restless shake of her head. "The usual maidenly dreams, nothing of value."

He gave a lift of his brow. "Having been born a tedious male, I fear I do not possess the secrets of mysterious maidenly dreams. What do they entail?"

"The typical desire for being beautiful and slaying gentlemen with a single glance. For taking London by storm and being the Toast of the Season." She grimaced. "For having a charming, handsome gentleman sweep one off to his castle to live in enchanted happiness."

"That is not such a bad dream, is it, Kate?" he murmured.

Her lips thinned as she considered her childish fantasies. "It is a dream that utterly depends upon another to offer happiness. I have come to realize that such a fate is never possible. I must seek my own fulfillment. My own dreams that can be accomplished by my own efforts."

She could feel him stiffen at her side. "And you hope to find fulfillment in defying your father, and in dreams while fluttering about London?"

Kate abruptly turned to face him with flashing eyes. She might have known. How could he possibly understand? He had not been constrained his whole life with impossible standards. He had not been smothered and imprisoned until he did not even recognize himself.

He had been free. Free to seek his dreams. Free to follow whatever path he desired.

Free to leave her to standing like a pathetic fool at the altar.

"It grows late," she retorted in chilled tones. "I must return to the hotel so that I may change for my drive with Lord Thorpe."

Not surprisingly, his features tightened at her firm command. But rather than offering the scathing lecture that was no doubt trembling upon the tip of his tongue, he instead forced a smile to his lips. At the same moment, his fingers tenderly caressed her cheek.

"Do you know, my sweet Kate, dreams are rather odd," he murmured in husky tones. "They are not a matter of choice but rather of destiny. You may hide and flee all you wish. In the end, it will be fate that determines your future. And not even you, my stubborn minx, can evade fate. Our fate. Together."

A shiver raced down her spine at the soft, relentless certainty in his voice.

He sounded as if he had actually seen the future. Their future.

No. That was ridiculous. No gentleman could see the future. Certainly not her future.

She was thinking mad thoughts.

He was mad.

Returning to the hotel, Kate had thankfully retreated to her chambers to change into a brilliant yellow riding gown and tailored black pelisse. Unfortunately, her thoughts refused to remain focused upon her upcoming meeting with Lord Thorpe. Or even upon her efforts to arrange her curls into a charming cluster atop her head.

Instead, she discovered herself brooding over and over upon Luce's parting shot.

Our fate. Together.

Blast it all. She had never claimed to comprehend

the muddled workings of the male mind. In fact, she had known for years that men in general were a mystery that appeared to defy logic.

Luce was simply a prime example of his bizarre species.

At least Lord Thorpe made a vague stab at normality, she told herself later, moving down the stairs and into the lobby to join the handsome nobleman as he awaited her beside a large potted plant.

She might not comprehend his mysterious interest in her, but at least he did not tangle her thoughts and twist her stomach into knots.

With a smile, Kate allowed the gentleman to politely lead her from the hotel toward the awaiting carriage. With that same delicate care, he lifted her onto the high-perch phaeton and she covertly studied his masculine body attired in a dove gray coat and pale ivory breeches with glossed Hessians.

Definitely a sight to make any maiden's heart flutter, she thought with a sigh of pleasure. And the perfect means of soothing her raw nerves.

Taking his own place upon the padded seat, Lord Thorpe gave a nod to his groom, who set the perfectly matched grays into motion. Only as they were rumbling away from the hotel did he turn to offer her his blinding smile.

"How are you feeling today?" he asked gently.

She grimaced, still feeling the lingering malaise clouding her mind. "As if I spent the evening in the ring with Gentleman Jackson."

"I feared as much." He reached out to lightly clasp her fingers. "Forgive me, Kate. I would never have ordered the champagne if I had known how quickly it would go to your head."

Kate allowed her fingers to remain in his grasp. There were none of the explosive tingles that she experienced when Luce touched her, but there was a pleasant warmth that she welcomed at the moment.

"It was not your fault," she assured him firmly. "I have never had champagne before, and I did not realize how much I was drinking until it was too late. By then, I no longer considered the dangers."

Perhaps sensing her lingering embarrassment at her night of overindulgence, he gave a low chuckle.

"You were charming."

"No, I made a fool of myself," she confessed, even if he was not to know just how foolish she had been. "Thank you for being a gentleman."

He shifted to face her as the dark eyes slowly roamed her pale features.

"It was not without its cost. You have no notion how long I paced in front of those damnable stairs, battling with the desire to say the hell with nobility and to join you upstairs."

Hoping he did not presume she was some sort of shallow tease, Kate gave a faint frown. "Forgive me. I did not intend to mislead you in any manner."

"Do not apologize, my dear." With a deliciously elegant gesture, he raised her fingers to his lips. "There is no rush to forward our relationship beyond what you desire. I am content to be companion, friend, and diversion. Whatever it is that you need."

Kate's smile swiftly returned at his light teasing. This man could no doubt charm the fish from the ocean.

"Is that a promise?"

"Yes," he said softly.

She raised her brows. "I will hold you to it, you know."

"I certainly hope so."

There was a wicked smokiness to his tone, but before Kate could respond, the carriage was slowing to turn into the already crowded park.

By mutual consent, their conversation turned to less intimate subjects, and Kate allowed herself to be entertained by his softly murmured descriptions of the various nobles who had remained in town rather than returning to their various estates. He possessed a wicked sense of humor and startling intelligence that soon had her chuckling at his antics. Slowly the lingering cobwebs in her head faded and she began to feel almost herself as they turned to wind their way back through the park.

At least now she knew what it felt like to be properly cast to the wind.

And wretchedly nursing a sore head.

And she did have the comfort of knowing she had not done anything to actually bring her shame.

No, a renegade voice whispered in the back of her mind, *you just begged two men to kiss you.*

And made a fool of yourself in front of Luce.

She fiercely thrust aside the distasteful thought. Those depressing notions were a thing of the past. Whether she had a glorious flirtation or not was incidental. There were an endless variety of experiences she had yet to seek and enjoy. And she was not going to waste her time brooding upon one mistake.

Breathing deeply of the astonishingly mild air, Kate settled back in her seat and watched as Lord Thorpe cast a lazy glance over the park. It was a lovely sight. For a maiden who had spent her entire life surrounded by flowers and trees and open fields it was not entirely pleasant to spend her days in cramped neighborhoods and among endless smoke-blackened buildings.

"The park seems rather empty," Lord Thorpe drawled as he turned back to regard her in an oddly piercing manner.

Kate gave a startled blink. Although there were no doubt far fewer society members in town than during the season proper, there were still a number of well-groomed citizens crowding the lanes.

"It seems quite bustling to me," she argued with a puzzled smile.

"Ah, but no chaperone."

"What?"

"Your personal, decidedly interfering guardian."

Comprehension dawned and she wrinkled her nose in wry amusement. "Oh."

He lifted a questioning brow at the soft color that suddenly warmed her cheeks. "You did not throttle him and toss his body into the Thames, did you?"

Kate took a moment to fully appreciate the lovely image, and then she gave a regretful shake of her head.

"No, although it is certainly a temptation."

He gave a laugh but there was a watchful intensity in the dark gaze. "I have already deduced that he is a rather close acquaintance. Is there anything else that I should know?"

Kate struggled to discourage her childish blush.

She was an intelligent, sophisticated, mature woman, she reminded herself. And intelligent, sophisticated, mature women did not blush like schoolgirls who had just experienced their first kiss.

A kiss they did not even recall.

"What do you mean?"

"Is he your lover?" Lord Thorpe came directly to the point.

"No," she denied, not having to pretend her

shocked tones. It was not always a simple matter to recall she was a supposedly experienced widow.

"He is very possessive of you."

"He considers himself responsible for me." Kate smiled with a hint of self-mockery. "And if you must know, he has a futile hope that he can wed me for my wealth."

The dark eyes narrowed. "That might explain his persistence. However, my dear, I do not believe that Lord Calfield has your fortune on his mind when he is looking at you."

"Lord Calfield always has my fortune on his mind. Or at least when he has not forgotten me utterly. Believe me, I am nothing more than a ready source of income."

"Then he is a fool," he murmured.

A fool? Kate gave a slow shake of her head. She had heard Luce called many things by both his friends and enemies.

Charming.

Rakish.

Ruthless.

Obsessed.

But never a fool.

"No, not a fool," she corrected. "A very dangerous and cunning gentleman."

There was a brief silence before Lord Thorpe abruptly leaned forward. "Shall I rid you of his presence?"

"Rid me of his presence?" Her eyes widened at the grim edge in his voice. "Good heavens. You sound like a character from a Gothic novel."

"Nothing so dramatic," he assured her, but there was no mistaking the sudden power she could sense about him. This was a man who could match Luce in ruthless determination, she recognized with a stab of surprise. Perhaps Luce had sensed that himself. It would certainly explain why he had taken such an illogical dislike toward a complete stranger. "But a few words in the right ears could ensure that his room at the hotel was no longer available and that his presence in London was far from comfortable."

"You could do that?" she demanded in surprise.

"Yes."

It was a temptation.

With Luce gone, she could enjoy herself without the ever-present knowledge he was plotting to sweep her back to Kent. And perhaps she could accept the attentions of Lord Thorpe without constantly comparing him to her aggravating ex-fiancé. But even as the thoughts swept through her mind, Kate was heaving a small sigh.

No.

To hide behind Lord Thorpe's obvious influence was no better than hiding behind her father's overbearing manner.

She was determined to face the world on her own.

And that included Lord Calfield.

"Knowing Luce, he would simply invade with his fleet of ships," she said dryly. "No, I think it best to ignore him. Eventually, he will have to seek out another victim. He must repair his fortunes soon."

Something that might have been disappointment rippled over his handsome face before he gave a nod of his head.

"As you wish. But remember, you can always turn to me if you need my assistance."

A warmth flowed through Kate at his kindness. She was honest enough to admit she had been initially attracted to him for his dark wicked beauty. A shallow, if typical, response. But she was discovering there was a great deal more to him than that.

"Thank you," she whispered, knowing that he did not make his promise lightly.

She also knew that if she were in trouble, she would gladly turn to this man.

Bless Lord Thorpe.

Damn Lord Thorpe.

Against all better sense, Luce had covertly followed Lord Thorpe's carriage as it drove off with Luce's own soon-to-be-bride. He was not certain what he intended to do. After all, he could hardly make a scene in the midst of the fashionable park. Not without driving Kate away for certain.

Still, he had known he could not simply await her return to the hotel. Not when she was in the clutches of a practiced rake.

It had been even worse than he dreaded.

His teeth had ground together at the sight of them gazing into each others' eyes like besotted fools. They were even holding hands despite the fact that they were seated in the midst of the entire *ton*.

It had taken all of Luce's considerable willpower not to gallop across the park and snatch Kate from the grasp of the treacherous beast.

Instead, he had turned his restless energy to more productive venues.

Kate desired to fulfill her fantasies? She desired dreams? Well, he would prove that he was more than capable of providing her with all the excitement she could desire.

With that thought grimly in mind, Luce had devoted his afternoon to weaving the perfect fantasy.

It had taken hours and a great deal of effort, but in the end he had been thoroughly satisfied.

He had one fantasy, made to order, that would satisfy the most demanding maiden.

In a considerably happier frame of mind, Luce changed into a pair of black breeches and dark claret coat. Brushing his golden hair in casual waves toward his freshly shaved countenance, he deemed himself ready and made his way to Kate's room.

He knocked on her door. There was a nerve-racking wait before Kate at last appeared, still wearing the lemon riding gown.

His heart skidded to a halt as he greedily drank in the sight of the vast amount of creamy skin exposed by the daring neckline.

He had promised himself he would take matters slowly. Kate was clearly an innocent. A babe among wolves, he acknowledged wryly. He would wait for her to indicate when she was prepared to begin her glorious flirtation.

But while his thoughts could nominate him for sainthood, his body was clearly in the gutter.

After spending the past twenty-four hours plagued with an aching frustration, he did not wish to take matters slowly. He wanted to scoop her in his arms and kiss those sweet lips. He wanted to slowly remove the pins from her hair and watch the satin fire drift about her shoulders.

Forcing himself to take a deep breath, Luce attempted to train his thoughts back to a more pure and noble path.

He was supposed to be fulfilling Kate's fantasies, not his own. Only then would she give up these foolish fancies and return to Kent as his wife.

"Are you ready?" he at last managed to inquire, his voice thankfully normal.

She lifted a cool brow, clearly not going weak in the knees at his presence.

"Ready for what?"

He swiftly dampened his instant annoyance and the not so small blow to his pride.

Her knees would grow weak soon enough, he assured himself.

But first . . . dinner.

"We are to have dinner tonight, do you not recall?"

"I recall you telling me we were having dinner," she corrected. "I do not recall agreeing."

"Come now, Kate," he urged with his most potent smile. "I have a surprise for you."

"A surprise?"

"You did want to try novel and daring things, did you not?"

She hesitated before curiosity at last got the better of her. "Very well, but I must change my gown first."

"No, you look perfect," Luce swiftly assured her, shifting uncomfortably.

Gads, he was already bothered by the indecent manner in which the gown was cut to reveal her snowy white shoulders. How the devil could he withstand the torture of lingering in the hall while she changed her gown just beyond the door?

Such a thing would encourage thoughts better left unthought.

Thankfully unaware of his discomfort, she gave a faint shrug. Then, slipping on a heavy satin cape and gloves, she followed him into the hall.

They walked in silence until Luce steered her past the lobby and out to the street, where a carriage awaited them.

"Where are we going?" she demanded as he handed her into the dark depths and swiftly settled beside her.

"First, a short drive," he informed her firmly, reaching up to rap against the roof of the carriage and send them into motion. Then, with great care, he reached for a blanket folded in the corner and placed it over her lap. "You must tell me if you become cold. We do not have far to go, but I do not wish you to catch a chill."

He could feel her startled gaze sweep over his profile as he ensured the warmed brick was next to her kidskin boots.

"I am quite comfortable, I thank you," she murmured. "And you needn't worry, I am never ill."

Luce settled back in his seat, readily meeting her searching gaze. He had never been the sort to fuss over another. Hardly surprising, considering he spent most days with hardened sailors who would bust his nose or worse at the least hint of fussing.

It came as a distinct surprise to discover he rather enjoyed treating Kate as if she were a rare and priceless object.

"I wish to worry over you, Kate. It gives me pleasure."

"Do you worry over me or my dowry?"

His lips twitched at her blunt question. Honesty was supposed to be refreshing, he reminded himself with wry humor. Unfortunately, "refreshing" was not precisely all that it was cracked up to be.

"You are oddly determined to consider me as no more than a fortune hunter, are you not, my dear?"

She gave a lift of her brow. "Do you blame me?"

"Well, I could point out that if all I desired was an easy means to wealth, there are no doubt any number of eager young chits filling the ballrooms I could chose from," he said with undeniable logic. "Unlike you, most maidens consider becoming a countess a goal worthy of any sacrifice. Even being wed to me."

In the dark, it was impossible to know if she blushed, but Luce sensed that he had struck a nerve.

"Then why are you here in this carriage with me rather than the ballrooms?" she demanded in sharp-edged tones. "It would obviously be a far more sensible, not to mention more profitable, use of your time."

Luce shifted so that he was fully facing her delicate profile. "Obviously. And yet here I am. That should prove something to you, Kate."

"That you do not enjoy having your will thwarted," she stubbornly insisted. "You decided that I was to be your wife and you refuse to concede defeat."

Bloody hell. Luce rolled his eyes heavenward. He should have his head examined. Being utterly crazed could be the only excuse for wasting his evening with a maiden so absurdly determined to hate him. A maiden, moreover, who was hurtling hell for leather down a path of ruin.

But crazed or not, he knew that he would have no other wife.

Miss Kate Frazer would be the Countess of Calfield. Regardless of how she might battle him along the way.

"I believe you are still overlooking the pertinent fact, my dear," he retorted in firm tones.

"And what fact would that be?"

"That I could have brought an end to this foolishness the moment I arrived in London." He caught and held her wary gaze with a steady determination.

"A brief message to your father would have you hauled back to Kent and condemned to your chambers until you are too old and feeble to leave them. I do not doubt that for all your brave words you would be relieved enough to accept my proposal in time, if only to escape your imprisonment."

Her breath caught, as if she were surprised by his sudden challenge of her bluff. Of course, she could not realize just how much she had revealed during her drunken confessions.

"Then why have you not done so?" she demanded.

He leaned against the leather seat, regarding her with a searching gaze. In the muted light, it was impossible to determine more than the stubborn set to her lovely jaw.

"Because I have come to believe that we can do better than a gentleman in need of a fortune and a maiden who feels compelled to please her father. With a bit of effort, I think that we can at least be friends."

"Friends?"

He gave a faint shrug. "Why not?"

There was a moment's pause, as if she were reluctantly considering words.

"You believe that I shall be more amenable to marriage if we are friends?" she at last demanded.

"Certainly that is my hope, and I will not insult your intelligence by pretending otherwise," he said in dry tones. "However, for the moment I am content to follow your lead and leave the future to unfold in its own time. All I ask is to simply be offered the opportunity to prove that I am not the unfeeling monster you perceive me to be."

She stiffened in surprise at his low words. "I have never thought you a monster, Luce."

"No?"

"Of course not. I . . . simply do not trust you."

"So you have told me." His gaze narrowed. "But you have not said why you will not offer me the opportunity to prove that you can place your faith in me. Do you fear that I might convince you that we belong together?"

She sucked in a sharp breath. "Certainly not."

"Good. Then we shall simply enjoy our time together while you are in London," he said in firm tones. "Without concern that I am plotting some devious and evil scheme to force you into marriage. A new beginning. Do you agree?"

A silence descended, broken only by the striking of hoofs against the cobbled road. Luce knew that Kate was far too intelligent not to realize he was still fiercely determined to have her as his wife. And yet, he had managed to manipulate her into either agreeing to his offer of friendship or allowing him to presume that she was frightened of being vulnerable to his charm.

An untenable notion for a woman with such pride.

"I will agree to accept your companionship if and when it pleases me," she at last reluctantly conceded. "But I will not be hounded nor bullied."

His low chuckle filled the carriage. "I will do my best to curtail my tendencies to hound and bully, which are always unforgivably gauche. Although I do not promise not to charm and bewitch. Two of my most potent weapons, I feel compelled to warn you."

Thankfully, her tension seemed to fade at his light teasing, and she even turned to offer him a faint smile.

"And whoever was foolish enough to convince

you that you possessed even the slightest ability to charm and bewitch?"

"Shall I offer you a list of references, my dear?" he murmured.

"Does it include more than just your mother, my lord?" she quipped.

"Ouch. A noteworthy hit." He laughed as the carriage slowed to a halt. "Thank heavens we have arrived."

She turned her head to peer out the window. "Arrived where?"

"You shall soon discover."

Pushing open the door before the groom could assist, Luce climbed out of the carriage, lowered the steps, and handed Kate onto the narrow walk. Not surprisingly, her brows lifted at the shabby buildings and the distinct aroma of rotting fish.

"The docks? This is your surprise?"

"Not quite." Pulling her arm through his own, he assisted her down the narrow steps that led toward the shadowed pier. In silence, they carefully traversed the slick wooden platform, halting as he came to the awaiting dinghy that floated upon the dark water. "Is all prepared, Foster?"

"Aye." A soft glow suddenly revealed the sailor as he lifted the shades from the lamp. "All is in order."

"Good." He glanced at his companion. "Shall we, my dear?"

Luce did not even realize that he held his breath until, after a short hesitation, Kate slowly gave a nod of her head, and he wrapped his arms about her to lift her into the boat. Heaving a silent breath of relief that she had not balked as he had half expected, he smoothly vaulted into the boat and settled Kate on the seat beside him. Even then, his sharp glance toward Foster silently urged the captain to set his oars in motion with all speed.

After no more than a low grunt, no doubt intended to reveal the older man's disapproval at hauling about a dreaded female, they were swiftly skimming over the water toward the silent ship looming in the distance.

Luce ignored the cantankerous Foster and instead turned his attention to the woman who was regarding him with a rather suspicious frown.

"Are you chilled?"

"No, the night is remarkably mild for November."

"And remarkably beautiful," he murmured. "We are blessed to be graced with starlight rather than fog."

His ploy to distract her seemed successful, as she obediently glanced up at the jewel-studded sky.

"It is beautiful."

"If you desire, I could dazzle you with my knowledge of the constellations."

"You must think I am easily dazzled," she said in wry tones.

"No, I think you are a very intelligent, discerning woman." He slowly smiled. "I do sense, however, that you would like to be dazzled."

She shrugged. "I just desire to enjoy myself."

"I can appreciate that." He tilted his head to one side. "Tell me, why have you never traveled to London before? Most young maidens have at least one season."

There was a pause before she at last gave a restless shrug. "My father considered it a waste of money."

"Money is hardly a concern for Sir Frazer," he prompted, wishing her to reveal the contents of her heart while she was not fuzzy with champagne. He needed to earn her trust if she was ever to willingly become his wife. "And he must have known that with your beauty and considerable dowry, you could have your choice of titled gentlemen."

"Obviously, he realized there was no need for such a journey when I could just as easily discover a titled gentleman in Kent."

He grimaced at her ready retort. She was not going to make this easy.

"A gentleman of his choice, as I have come to discover, not your own."

She offered another shrug. "My father has rarely considered anyone's desires but his own. Like most gentlemen, he does not believe a woman is capable of knowing her own mind."

He leaned closer, his expression somber. "It is not entirely fair to presume every gentleman believes such nonsense, Kate. There are any number who not only appreciate the female mind, but consider it a prime asset in a wife."

"Gentlemen such as you?" she demanded in disbelieving tones.

"Yes. I would certainly hope that the mother of my children would possess the qualities I hope to instill in my heirs."

"What qualities?"

"Intelligence, courage, and an independent spirit," he promptly listed. "Only a fool would believe a weak, clinging wife could produce such offspring."

He seemed to catch her off guard, and for a moment she searched his features in the silvery moonlight.

"But surely you must have considered me weak and clinging when you first met me?"

Luce carefully considered his words. Any hint of

attempting to deceive her would ensure she never believed another word he offered.

"I thought you reserved and somewhat uncomfortable in my presence, but to be honest, I presumed your father was responsible for your demure manner. He is overpowering in even the smallest doses." He allowed a shudder to race through his body. "That did not, however, prevent me from noting your well-educated conversation and the ability to confront a near stranger as your fiancé without giggling or fainting or giving in to hysterics. That reveals more courage than if you had confronted me with sword in hand." A wry smile suddenly curved his lips. "And of course, during the past few days, I have been charmingly convinced of your independent spirit."

"Hardly charmingly, I would think."

He gave a soft chuckle. "Well, at least unmistakably."

"Yes, I suppose."

"It is an independence I greatly admire, considering you were raised by a father who does not seem to appreciate women of spirit," he said firmly. "I know from experience how difficult it can be to oppose a parent's desire to mold you into something that you are not."

She regarded him with disbelief, not seeming to notice the steady pull of oars was slowing as they neared the looming ship.

"You?"

"Yes, me."

"I find that hard to believe," she retorted with a shake of her head.

"Why?"

"To begin with, you are male. Sons, especially heirs, are always considered perfect no matter how flawed they might be."

"Wrong," he informed her, reaching out to tweak one of the burnished curls that had escaped her bonnet. "My father never bothered to hide his frustration that I was not destined to become the polished rake and gambler he thought it necessary for a nobleman to be. It did not help matters that I readily challenged his determination to toss away his entire fortune upon the card tables. In fact, he commanded me to leave the estate when I turned eighteen."

He thought he heard her breath catch. "I . . . forgive me, Luce. I did not know."

Very few people did know.

Luce rarely spoke of those black days when he and his father had waged endless battles. Nor did he speak of the manner in which his mother had taken to her bed, leaving him to face the burden of their mounting debts. Of the nights he had walked the floor wondering what he could do to prevent disaster. Not even of his relief when his father had tossed him out the door so that he no longer was forced to watch the inevitable ruin.

He far preferred others to believe him arrogant and imperious rather than reveal the uncertain lad who had fought to survive because he simply was too frightened to give up.

Tonight, however, it felt somehow right to share his past with this woman.

"I was fortunate to possess a small allowance from my grandmother that kept me afloat and eventually helped me to establish my business." He breathed in deeply of the salt-scented air. "In truth, I was perhaps the most content I had ever been. For the first time I was in utter control of my life with no concerns beyond keeping my ships afloat. And then . . ."

"Your father died and you became Earl of Calfield," she finished softly, surprisingly reaching out to lightly touch his arm.

A poignant warmth flowed through his blood. It was the first occasion she had sought to touch him of her own will.

"Yes."

"It must have been difficult to accept a title you did not desire," she murmured with startling perception.

He grimaced. "I will admit that I considered taking one of my ships and sailing so far away that no one could ever find me again." He paused as he searched her beautiful features bathed in silver light. "Now I am very happy I did nothing so foolish."

"I cannot imagine why," she muttered. "It sounds delightful to me."

"But if I were hiding among the savage natives, I would not be here with you." He stroked the softness of her cheek. "And at this moment, there is nowhere else on earth I would rather be."

"Luce . . ."

"Ah, we are here." Waiting for Foster to maneuver them next to the ship, he offered his companion a small smile. "I hope you are prepared for your surprise?"

CHAPTER SIX

Nothing could have prepared Kate for the sight that greeted her.

Wide-eyed, she gazed at the torches that circled the large blanket spread on the bow of the ship. Upon the blanket were platter after platter of delectable foods with countless flowers sprinkled across it all.

Set in the midst of the star-sprinkled night, it was mysterious and beautiful. Like something out of a dream.

"What do you think?" he whispered close to her ear.

She lifted glittering eyes to meet his expectant smile. "It is . . . lovely."

"Here."

With a tug on her hand he settled her on the blanket. Swiftly, he lowered himself close beside her and Kate was suddenly aware of the scent of warm male skin mingling with the perfume of flowers.

She knew she should scoot away and put a sensible amount of distance between them. But an odd sense of ease had been woven between them over the past few moments. A connection that hummed in the air and soothed the warning voices in the back of her mind. It seemed somehow right to have him so close to her side.

"I have tried to think of a variety of foods you were most likely not to have tried before," he told her, taking a plate and beginning to fill it with the bounty before them. "Escargots. Fois gras. Quail eggs with caviar. Eggplant and, last, papaya."

"Dear heavens," she breathed as she accepted the plate. "It is a feast."

"A feast for the senses." The blue gaze swept over her features, lingering a tantalizing moment on her lips. "Just as you requested."

A renegade flare of pleasure warmed her heart as she considered the effort that Luce had taken to create such a special setting. No one had ever concerned themselves with pleasing her. Certainly not in such a spectacular style.

The knowledge that he must have devoted hours, and a not inconsiderable amount of his limited income, threatened to undermine her determination to treat him with utter indifference.

With an effort, she turned her attention to the food awaiting her approval. Food seemed far preferable to the unwelcome pang of tenderness.

In silence she savored the rich, varied tastes, occasionally sipping from the wine, although she was careful to ensure it was only tiny sips. She felt him watching her. Perhaps judging whether his efforts had succeeded in soothing his crazed, unpredictable fiancée, she wryly acknowledged. But she refused to allow herself to be bothered by the unwavering scrutiny. Instead, she thoroughly savored the meal.

She had cleaned the plate before she set it aside with a satisfied sigh.

"That was delicious," she murmured.

"Which one?"

"All of them." She lifted her head to meet his

indulgent smile, not even flinching when he carefully wiped her lips with a linen napkin. "I cannot believe that I waited so long to try such wonderful dishes."

"There is much more to try. Lobster, curry from India, fresh asparagus made by a top French chef . . ."

"Not tonight," she protested with a chuckle. In truth, she did not believe that she could stuff in one more morsel.

"No, not tonight," he agreed, leaning on one elbow and tilting his head to one side. "I presume that your father prefers the more traditional English dishes?"

"My father is suspicious of anything beyond roasted venison and boiled potatoes," she retorted in dry tones. "He believes that sauces and confections are a plot of the French to overthrow our monarchy."

He laughed softly at her confession. "Good gads, venison and boiled potatoes? It is no wonder you were starving for something different."

"Yes." Her gaze slowly moved about the velvet darkness that surrounded them. In the distance, a lone bird sang to the stars, its song oddly haunting in the deep silence. "Although I did not realize that I was starving until it was almost too late. Now I am determined never to seclude myself from such pleasures again."

His gaze became watchful, as if he were not entirely pleased by her soft words.

"You seem to have forgotten that there is more than mere pleasure in life, and that you managed to accomplish a great deal while you were in Kent, my dear. Surely you take pride in having built an orphanage and ensuring that the school was opened to the local girls? No small feats for a young maiden."

It was true enough. She was proud of what she had accomplished. How could she not be?

Because of her, dozens of children had been saved from the coal mines and workhouses. And it was only at her relentless insistence that the vicar had agreed to allow the village girls to attend his daily lessons.

Even a woman utterly devoid of conceit would have taken a measure of satisfaction in the thought that she had truly made a difference in the neighborhood.

"I suppose so," she slowly admitted.

"You possess a rare talent to not only realize the plight of those less fortunate, Kate, but also to take charge and ensure you do all in your power to make their existence better," he murmured in insistent tones. "Most among society prefer to turn their heads and pretend that they do not notice those in need."

She gave a small shrug. "There are many who contribute to worthy causes."

"Contribute funds, not their hearts." He regarded her steadily. "Only you have been willing to take on such formidable tasks. It is a gift that you should not take for granted."

"But it is not enough," she stated firmly. "I realize that now."

A small silence fell at her determined words. Then he reached out to lightly stroke a curl from her cheek.

"So what do you intend to do, Kate?"

She gave a blink of surprise at his unexpected question. "Do?"

"For your future."

"Oh." She shrugged. "I do not intend to consider the future for now. I will worry about tomorrow when it comes."

A frown tugged at his brow as his fingers shifted to her chin and raised her face so he could closely study her set expression.

"You cannot remain in London indefinitely. Your father is bound to discover your deception sooner or later."

"I realize that, but while I am here, I am going to appreciate my independence," she insisted, refusing to apologize for her impulsive desires.

And why should she apologize? she asked herself sternly.

She had waited a lifetime for this brief period of freedom. Surely she deserved to take her pleasure without explaining herself to a gentleman who desired only to return her to the shackles she had fled?

"And what if this outlandish scheme of yours brings you ruin?" he demanded.

She met his gaze squarely. "At the moment, it is a risk that I am willing to take. If you are concerned for your own reputation in being associated with me, you are quite welcome to return to Kent."

Despite his best intentions, Luce could not entirely hide his flare of exasperation.

Understandable, she told herself with a spark of dry amusement. He was a gentleman accustomed to giving orders and having them obeyed.

It was a small miracle and a testament to his desperation that he had forced himself to maintain his dubious patience.

"I cannot believe you would be content to live in shamed isolation because of a brief bout of insanity."

Kate considered his accusing words for a long moment.

"No, I intend to take great care that I do not cause a scandal," she at last conceded. "But to be honest, I have lived in isolation with or without shame. And if worse does come to worse then I will discover some means of caring for myself. I do possess an independent allowance from my mother, and more importantly, I no longer depend upon others to protect me from the world."

Her words did little to reassure him and he gave a slow shake of his golden head.

"It would be a sin against nature to have you waste into a spinster, Kate. You were meant to be a wife and mother."

Kate felt her own annoyance being stirred to life.

She had been honest with Luce. Far more honest than she had intended to be, thanks to her bout of vulnerability at his own confessions of his childhood and the beautiful dinner he had created.

She did not desire to be reminded that his only concern was luring her to the nearest church.

"You mean I was meant to be *your* wife, do you not, Luce?" she demanded tartly.

His mouth thinned. "Yes."

"I have told you that . . ."

"Very well. You have made yourself gruesomely clear, Kate," he murmured, the annoyance seeming to drain from the blue eyes to be replaced with a dark, far more dangerous amusement. "I do not desire to ruin this evening with an argument. Not when there are far more pleasant means of passing the time."

Kate shivered, suddenly aware of their isolation. They might have been completely alone on the ship. Just one man and one woman with the seductive beauty of the starlit night.

"And precisely what pleasant means are you referring to?" she demanded with a lift of her brows.

"Well, I could offer a few suggestions . . ."

"No," she interrupted in a voice that was oddly husky. "That is quite all right."

"Then you tell me what you wish to do," he urged softly.

A voice in the back of her mind warned her to simply demand to be taken back to her hotel. It was without a doubt the wisest choice to make.

Unfortunately, she felt too restless to simply return to her chambers for the evening. Not when the night was so mild, and the view so spectacular.

And her companion so tantalizing, a wicked voice whispered in the back of her mind.

She gave an unconscious shake of her head and rushed to divert the unwelcome thought.

"Tell me of your travels," she abruptly demanded. "Have you visited many exotic locations?"

A golden brow lifted in mild surprise, but thankfully, he leaned back on his hands and allowed his gaze to wander over the large ship.

"I have been to Jamaica, the West Indies, and even to the colonies. I suppose some might consider them exotic."

"They must have been fascinating." She tilted her head to one side. "I have heard that the air in the West Indies smells of spice and flowers. Is it true?"

He gave a wry chuckle. "Actually the air smelled of tar and sweaty men and rotting fish."

A hint of disappointment fluttered over the delicate features. "Really?"

"Well, to be honest, I rarely visited more than the docks and warehouses, which are tediously similar the world over. As are seedy taverns and rat-infested inns."

She wrinkled her nose at his blunt honesty. "You do not make it sound particularly romantic."

"Forgive me." He offered a rueful smile. "I fear that I am destined never to be invited for a series of lectures throughout London."

"Not if you intend to discuss seedy taverns and rat-infested inns," she readily agreed.

"Very well, I shall attempt to leave out any mention of lice and rats and food that an Englishman would consider unfit for his hounds."

"It could not have been all bad."

He paused for a moment, his expression oddly softening in the moonlight.

"No. Although I have yet to discover a land as beautiful as England, there is nothing to compare to nights upon the waves with the stars splattered like diamonds across the sky and the silence so profound that you can hear your very soul." He breathed in deeply. "It is those moments that lure men to the sea."

Kate caught her breath at the near poetry of his soft words. "Do you still sail?"

"Not as often as I would desire." He turned his head to meet her gaze. "It was a simple matter when I possessed only the *Windsong*. Now I cannot afford to be away from London for months at a time. Not without one disaster or another occurring."

"But you miss your time at sea?"

"Very much."

Kate absently tucked her feet beneath her, a wistful smile tugging at her lips. "You are most fortunate, you know. It must be glorious to simply sail away without knowing what you might see or discover. Every day would be a fresh adventure."

"Some days are more adventurous than others, considering the treachery of the seas, and the determination of pirates," he said dryly. "Still, there are few places I would rather be."

"Yes." She heaved a faint sigh, quite easily able to imagine drifting into the darkness with no concerns, no petty rules, and nothing but the unknown horizon to occupy her mind. "I envy you, Luce."

There was a slight pause before she heard a faint rustle, and then warm fingers were gently pressing her chin up to meet a pair of glittering blue eyes.

"You wish to travel?"

"I can imagine nothing I would enjoy more," she retorted without hesitation.

"You do realize that I could make such a dream possible, my dear?" he aked softly. "I have only to say the word and we could be cast off and headed for wherever your heart may desire."

Her breath caught in her throat at his mesmerizing words. Wherever her heart desired? Simple words, and yet unexpectedly poignant.

"You make it sound very simple," she murmured.

"What could be more simple?" he demanded. "For now, your father believes you to be in Surrey, and those in London know you only as a lonely widow. There would be no one to halt you from indulging your dreams."

For a moment, she allowed the tempting image of sand-scoured Egypt and lush Greece to rise to her mind. It would indeed be a dream come true. To walk in the footsteps of the ancients, and stand among the ruins of past civilizations. To perhaps even travel to distant lands with their savage natives and vast wilderness.

Then she was ruefully thrusting aside temptation. Luce had already warned her that every adventure came with a price. A throbbing head had been the cost of overindulgence with champagne. The cost of sailing off with Luce would be much greater.

A cost she was not yet prepared to pay.

She pulled from his lingering touch with a lift of her chin. "A tempting offer, Luce, but one I fear I must decline."

"Why?"

"I prefer to remain in London."

He gave a slow shake of his head. "No."

"What?"

"It is not because you prefer to remain in London," he said with relentless assurance. "It is because you are frightened to take the risk."

Her eyes swiftly narrowed in annoyance. "That is absurd. Why would I be frightened?"

His gaze slowly swept over her shadowed countenance. "Because you fear that you might discover more than distant lands."

"And what would that be?"

"What every person desires. Friendship. Passion. Love. The certainty that you possess a companion who will forever stand by your side."

A sharp tingle raced down her spine at his confident words. He was so utterly certain. So convinced that he could read her heart.

It was more than a tad unnerving.

"I think that we should return to the hotel," she abruptly announced, determinedly pressing herself to her feet before he could discover some means of undermining her decision.

Unfortunately, her haste was her undoing. Even as she rose, her foot remained caught upon the hem of her gown, and with a stifled gasp she discovered herself tumbling forward.

Moving with smooth grace, Luce was before her, catching her in his arms to keep her upright.

"Careful, my love," he murmured, holding her far too close for Kate's peace of mind.

Clutching at the lapels of his coat, Kate sternly willed her knees to halt their urge to give out. A task that was far more difficult than it should have been.

"You may release me," she forced herself to mutter.

"In a moment." His head lowered, his cheek softly brushing over her curls.

"Luce . . ."

She felt his lips touch her temple as he breathed in deeply. "Kate, what is that perfume you wear?"

Her toes curled at the seductive rasp in his voice. Or perhaps it was the heat of his body that surrounded her like a cloak of temptation.

"I . . . I wear no perfume," she inanely retorted. "It is merely my soap."

"No. It is you. The scent of you," he muttered, his arms tightening about her body. "I would know it anywhere. It is driving me mad."

She shivered at the fierce, unexpected excitement that raced through her blood. She wanted to remain in his arms. To tug his head downward and press her lips to his own. To experience the magic that beaconed.

Instead, with an unsteady motion, she forced her hands to push at his broad chest. Luce's particular brand of magic was far more potent than she could ever have expected.

Rather to her disappointment, he reluctantly lowered his arms and stepped back to regard her with darkened eyes.

"Do you expect me to apologize?"

No doubt she should be embarrassed by what just occurred between them.

Or angry.

Or even shocked.

But what she felt instead was an odd sense of awareness. As if some deep, unrealized question had finally been answered.

It was as unexplainable as it was confusing, and with a vague shake of her head, Kate wrapped her arms protectively about her slender waist.

"No."

"Good." His lips slowly curled in a smile. "Because I am not at all repentant. I enjoy having you in my arms. Just as I enjoy having you in my company. And I will continue to attempt to convince you that we belong together."

"I . . . we must return to the hotel," she said abruptly.

He paused for a long moment before giving a mysterious smile. "If that is what you wish."

Kate clenched her teeth. The trouble was she did not know if that was what she wished at all.

And it was entirely Lord Calfield's fault.

This was entirely Kate's fault.

Not only had she ensured that he would devote another restless night to pacing his chambers. A far too frequent occurrence. But now he was near to an open battle with his most staunch friend.

He stood in the sitting room of his hotel chambers, crumpling the list of eligible maidens that he held in his fist and glaring at the man who had arrived with the dawn.

"Dammit, Foster, I asked you to discover what you could of Lord Thorpe, not to play matchmaker.

Why the devil would I desire the names of rich maidens when I already possess a perfectly suitable fiancée?"

Calmly sipping the coffee that Luce had ordered, the hardened sailor merely lifted a brow. As always, he managed to appear as if he had slept in his clothes and forgotten to shave. A man perfectly suited for his life at sea.

"I know what was requested," the sailor retorted as he settled more comfortably in the chair. "But after last night, I decided that you were more in need of a bit of common sense."

"What the bloody hell is that supposed to mean?"

Foster carefully set aside his cup, as if sensing he might have need of his fists. A wise choice, considering Luce was already battling his frustrated desires and sleepless nights.

"It means that last night I wasn't liking what I was seeing. No man worth his salt would. That woman has you behaving daft."

Luce slowly narrowed his gaze. "Daft?"

"I seen how eagerly you seek to please her." Frowning, Foster regarded him with a somber expression. "She has you behaving no better than a mincing dandy."

A flare of annoyance raced through Luce. As much from the disdainful manner in which Foster spoke of Miss Frazer as from the implication that he was an overeager twit. He would not endure any disrespect toward his future wife. Not from anyone.

"As I recall, you were the one to warn that I did not possess enough concern for Miss Frazer's tender sensibilities. You even predicted her reaction to being left at the altar," he said in sharp-edged tones. "Why do you quibble now that I have discovered the truth of your concerns?"

A further hint of color touched the already ruddy countenance. "It is one thing to offer the wench a measure of respect, 'tis quite another to allow her to dangle you upon a hook like a landed trout."

"First a mincing dandy and now you compare me to a trout?" Luce demanded in dangerous tones.

"Can you deny that she has you chasing after her as if you were a beggar?" Foster demanded stiffly. "She should be pleased to become your wife. Any other maiden would be."

Luce grimaced at the blunt accusation. He did have his pride, after all. A great deal of pride.

Still, he had come to realize that wedding him was not nearly the prize he had presumed it to be. At least not for Kate. He would have to do whatever necessary to convince her that he was the only gentleman who could truly bring her happiness.

Surely that was not such a horrid sacrifice?

"I was mistaken to take Miss Frazer for granted, Foster. And even more mistaken to have humiliated her in such a public fashion." He paced to glance down at the tidy garden that was annoyingly empty of Kate's presence. "She is more than merely an easy means to a fortune. She is a young maiden who deserves to be wooed by a gentleman who truly cares for her happiness."

Not surprisingly, the confirmed bachelor recoiled in distaste at the mention of wooing a proper maiden.

"Gads, it is as I feared. You begin to sound like some lackwitted poet," Foster bemoaned with a visible shudder. "You have been ashore too long. It softens the mind of even the most sensible gentleman."

"I assure you that my wits are in perfect working order."

"No." A stubborn expression settled on the wide features. "If that were true, then you would have changed your bait and gone after easier prey days ago."

Luce was glad that his arms were safely locked across his chest. Otherwise he might very well have attempted to shake his friend. As it was, he contented himself with a glare of exasperation.

"We both know I cannot afford to lose this particular prey. Not unless I desire to watch my estate crumble into ruin."

"One quarry is much like another. No use bemoaning the one that got away."

Luce snapped his brows together at the muttered accusation. "She has not gotten away. Not by a long shot."

As if regretting stirring Luce's ire, the older man lifted his hand in a soothing manner.

"I did not mean to imply you could not have her if you desired. I merely wonder why you would go to the effort."

"I should think that was obvious."

"Why?"

For a moment Luce was at a loss for words. He knew that Kate was meant to be his wife. It was a truth written within his soul.

Unfortunately, he knew that to confess such a thing would only convince Foster for certain he had lost his wits.

"She suits me."

Foster lifted a bushy brow. "There are bound to be any number of women in London who would suit you just as well. And with far less effort."

"Tell me, Foster, do you have some reason to dislike Miss Frazer?" he abruptly demanded.

Just for a moment, Luce thought his friend might

refuse to answer. In obvious discomfort, Foster scratched his head before at last clearing his throat.

"Truth be told, I think the chit is playing you for a fool, and I haven't a hankering to listen to you blubbering over a damnable broken heart."

Well.

That was unexpected.

Luce blinked in startled disbelief at the weathered countenance. "Good God, are you foxed?"

Foster folded his arms over his chest, clearly embarrassed at having confessed his inner thoughts.

"No, I damn well am not foxed. And neither am I blind. I seen how you looked at that woman."

"Of course I looked. For God's sakes, what man with blood in his veins wouldn't look?"

"It wasn't the look of a man wanting a taste of a pretty lass."

"I assure you that I very much desired a taste."

Foster stubbornly gave a shake of his head. "You've lusted after plenty women afore. You never gazed at them as if you had found a precious treasure you feared might be stolen."

Luce stiffened. Dash it all. Foster was being absurd. Precious treasure, indeed.

If he had gazed at Kate, it had been as a gentleman at the end of his patience. Nothing else.

"I possess a measure of fondness for Miss Frazer," he at last admitted in a tight voice. "But I am certainly in no danger of becoming the pathetic wretch you have described."

Annoyingly, Foster merely offered a grunt at his reassuring words. "If that is true, then there is nothing to keep you from at least having a go at some of them females on the list. I have it from a lady friend of mine that all of them are proper enough, with a fat dowry to tempt any man. And all more than eager to welcome the attentions of an earl. You could be wed afore the ink dries on the license."

Luce's nose flared at the mere thought. "Dammit, Foster, I do not want to wed another."

"But . . ."

"No. I do not care if they all come with dowries the size of France and bells upon their toes. I have chosen Miss Frazer to be my wife, and that is precisely who I will have."

"Aye." Foster thinned his lips until they nearly disappeared. "And what if she will not have you?"

Luce sucked in a sharp breath, abruptly turning toward the window. He would not even consider the possibility of defeat.

It was untenable.

"I would request, Foster, that unless you are interested in acquiring a lovely young debutante as a bride for yourself, you would devote less attention to making lists and instead discover the information that I requested upon Lord Thorpe."

He could feel Foster's gaze boring into his back, but as Luce refused to turn and confront the unwelcome concern upon the craggy features, he at last heaved a heavy sigh.

"Aye, sir."

CHAPTER SEVEN

When the knock came upon her door early the next morning, Kate offered considerable thought to whether or not to simply ignore it. She had already received her breakfast tray and Lord Thorpe was far too much of a gentleman to brazenly approach her private chambers.

By means of rather simple deduction, it left only Lord Calfield as the possible culprit standing on the other side of the wooden panels.

For long moments she wavered. She was not at all certain that she was prepared to confront the charming, fiercely determined gentleman at such an early hour. Not when she had yet to finish her tea.

Still, the discreet but insistent pounding showed no indication of ending anytime before the next century. If she did not answer, then there was bound to be unwelcome notice. She would prefer that the entire hotel not be speculating upon Mrs. Freemont and her gentlemen callers.

Heaving a faint sigh, she rose to her feet and unconsciously smoothed the skirts of her deep rose gown. She even paused before the mirror to adjust her curls before she realized what she was doing.

"For goodness' sakes, Kate, do not be any more of a fool than you need to be," she sternly chastised herself. What did it matter if she were attired in rags with her hair in tangles? She had no desire to attract the attentions of the annoying gentleman. Indeed, she had attempted to do precisely the opposite.

With a small sniff at her ridiculous behavior, she firmly marched to pull open the door. She even managed to paste a smile to her lips, although it promptly disappeared as her mouth dropped open in shock.

"Julia." She gave a slow, disbelieving shake of her head.

"Thank goodness you are here," the young maiden breathed, brushing by the frozen Kate to stand in the center of the room.

Closing the door, Kate turned and regarded her cousin with a wide gaze. Although she had sent Julia a discreet note when she had first arrived in London offering her location in the case of dire need, she had never expected her young cousin to suddenly appear.

Indeed, she could not imagine any reason for Julia to be here unless . . . she abruptly pressed a hand to her clenched stomach.

"Julia, what is it?" she demanded, her heart lodged in her throat. "Has something occurred? Is it Father?"

"Hold, Kate." Julia put up her hands with a reluctant smile. "Your father and family are well."

"Oh." Kate heaved a deep sigh of relief. "Thank God."

"Do not thank the heavenly father so swiftly," Julia warned with a grimace. "I fear that you will not be at all pleased with what I have to tell you."

Assured that at least nothing horrid had befallen, Kate waved a hand toward the nearby sofa. "Then I suppose you should have a seat and tell me what brings you to London."

With a faint nod, Julia removed her bonnet and settled upon the edge of the cushions. She waited for Kate to settle beside her before drawing in a deep breath.

"Kate, your father is in London," she abruptly announced.

For the second time in mere minutes, Kate felt her mouth drop in shock. "In . . . London?"

Reaching out, Julia gently grasped her hand in her own. "Yes. It seems that he received a message from his man of business concerning an investment he is particularly interested in."

Of course, it was not unheard of for her father to visit London. He had often done so over the years, although he had sternly refused Kate's persistent pleas to be taken along. Still, it was truly the height of ill fortune that he would choose to make one of his infrequent visits at this precise moment.

Stunned by the unexpected development, Kate swallowed the lump that threatened to form in her throat.

"When did he arrive?"

"Last evening."

"I . . . see." It was a struggle to clear her fogged mind enough to think coherently. Her father. In London. Dear heavens. "How long does he intend to remain?"

"Only a week." Julia grimaced, her lovely eyes filled with rueful amusement. "You know how your father can be. I swear he complained the entire trip that he would not remain a moment longer than necessary in such a wretched place. If it were not for the fact he believes that he is about to make yet another fortune, he would never have set foot in what he claims to be 'the cauldron of wickedness and vice.'"

Against her will, Kate felt her lips twitch at Julia's resigned tone. Her father had always held London and society in contempt. She could only presume that it had something to do with her mother and the torrid affair that had led her to Paris.

The brief amusement, however, was swift to fade as she met her cousin's concerned gaze. "Well, it is certainly inconvenient, but surely there is no need to panic. Father is not likely to set foot outside his hotel unless it is to visit his man of business and—"

"I have not finished, Kate," Julia interrupted, her pretty countenance rueful. "Your father did not come to London alone."

Kate gave a lift of her brows at the ridiculous words. Of course her father did not come alone. Not only had Julia obviously traveled with him, but Sir Frazer never left his estate without a battalion of servants, stewards, and solicitors. In truth, his long train of coaches was more suited to royalty than a mere "sir."

"I suppose your mother is also here?" she retorted.

"She is, along with Aunt Sylvia and her endless brood of children, Cousin Mary and her two daughters, as well as Cousin Henry."

Kate slowly leaned back in the cushions, stomach churning with disbelief. "Saints above. Whatever are they all doing here?"

Julia heaved a sigh. "Well, Aunt Sylvia decided that it was high time her tribe of savages were allowed to view the numerous historical sights, which might very well prove the end of refined civilization. Cousin Mary is determined to purchase wardrobes for her daughters, as if one seamstress is not like another, and Cousin Henry claims he desires a new pair of Hessians, although it is my opinion that he has more of an interest in the local brothels than in the boot maker."

Kate's stomach clenched a bit tighter. This was a disaster. A stroke of ill fortune of monumental proportions.

Avoiding her father was merely a matter of caution. After all, he could be depended upon to avoid any location that might possibly attract members of the *ton*. But to avoid dozens of relatives complete with their hordes of servants who would obviously be crawling throughout the streets of London . . .

"Blast," she muttered, clenching her hands in her lap.

Julia offered a sympathetic sigh. "I am sorry, Kate. But I had to warn you."

"Of course. Can you imagine what would have happened had I accidentally bumped into Aunt Sylvia upon the street?" She gave a sudden shudder.

"No doubt you would discover yourself hauled back to Kent and locked in the cellar before you knew what had occurred," Julia retorted.

The melodramatic words should have been humorous. Kate, however, did not laugh.

While her father might not actually lock her in a cellar, she knew him well enough to realize that what little breath of independence she had managed to wrangle would be gone forever. He would see her deception as a flagrant attempt to follow in the footsteps of her mother and would take firm action to ensure that she was never allowed another moment alone.

He might even decide to buy her another fiancé. One that would arrive at the church on time.

She sucked in a sharp breath at the ghastly thought. No. She could not allow it to happen. She would not.

"Obviously, I must ensure that I am not discovered," she muttered in low tones.

"How?"

"I suppose I have only two choices," Kate grudgingly admitted. "I can either return home or remain in these chambers until Father leaves. Neither of which is particularly pleasant to contemplate."

"Which will you do?"

Kate turned her head to regard the tidy but cramped sitting room. The mere thought of being confined in such a small space was enough to make her cringe. Surely an entire week of pacing the floors would be unbearable. And yet, she was not at all prepared to return to Kent and her life of relentless boredom.

"I do not know," she admitted with a sigh. "It would be a wrench to leave London."

"You are enjoying your stay, then?" Julia demanded.

"How could I not?" Kate gave a lift of her hands. "I could never have dreamed of all the wondrous sights and endless entertainments. I believe I could remain here for months and never grow weary."

A teasing smile touched her cousin's lips. "And what of your wish for a glorious flirtation? Have you encountered any dashing, delightful rogues?"

Caught off guard, Kate could feel the revealing heat crawl beneath her skin. "Actually, I . . . there has not been much time."

A hint of stubborn determination hardened Julia's delicate features. "Oh no. There is something you are not telling me. Who is he?"

Kate nervously cleared her throat. "Well, there is Lord Thorpe. And before you begin torturing me with a dozen questions, allow me to inform you that I know very little about him beyond the fact that he is handsome, charming, and a true gentleman."

Oddly, Julia narrowed her gaze at the rushed words. Or perhaps, not so oddly. After all, the two girls had been raised practically as sisters since Julia's mother had come to live with Sir Frazer after the abrupt departure of Kate's mother. She always knew when Kate was attempting to hide something from her.

"There is something else," she said in stern tones. "Give over, Kate."

Just for a moment Kate battled against the inevitable, and then with a sigh, she offered Julia a faint grimace.

"Lord Calfield discovered that I had traveled to London and followed me here."

A stunned silence descended as Julia pressed a hand to her heart. "Dear heavens. How do you know? Has he approached you?"

Kate gave a decidedly humorless laugh. "Oh yes. In fact, he is staying at this very hotel."

"Here? But this is terrible."

"Fairly terrible, yes."

Her cousin gave a slow shake of her head. "I cannot believe it. He did come to Rosehill, of course, but when I told him that you were in Surrey and had no desire to speak with him, I presumed that he had chosen to accept your decision. I never dreamed . . . however did he find you?"

Kate shrugged. "He merely followed the tracks I thought I had hidden so cleverly. Obviously not cleverly enough."

Brooding upon the unexpected revelation, Julia puckered her brow, clearly attempting to sift through the numerous difficulties that Luce's presence in London would present.

"Does he know of your charade?"

"Unfortunately, yes."

"But he has not exposed you?"

"Not as of yet." Ridiculously, Kate felt her blush deepen. She discovered herself oddly reluctant to discuss Luce and his determined pursuit. "He believes that if he is charming enough, I will eventually come to my senses and return to Kent to be his wife."

The dark brows lifted in astonishment. "And is he?"

"Is he what?"

"Charming?"

"Do not be absurd," Kate retorted with more force than necessary. Perhaps because she was telling such a blatant falsehood. If nothing else, Luce possessed the charm of the devil himself. "At the moment, I am forced to endure his presence. Soon enough he will grow weary and search out a more willing maiden."

"Well. This is an awkward predicament. And more than a bit dangerous, Kate. Lord Calfield could easily ruin your reputation if he chose, you know." Julia eyed her with obvious concern. "Are you certain that it would not be best simply to return to Kent?"

"Actually, I am uncertain of anything at the moment, Julia," Kate ruefully conceded. "I must have time to consider what is for the best."

"Well, do not do anything without informing me of your decision," Julia warned in firm tones, rising to her feet. "We are staying at the King's Arms. Leave a message for me there."

Kate also rose, giving a nod of her head. "Very well."

"I must go before my absence is noted." Julia leaned forward to place a light kiss upon Kate's cheek. "But know that I am here for you if you have need."

Kate smiled fondly at the maiden who had always provided her with unquestioning love and support.

"Thank you, Julia."

"For goodness' sakes, take care of yourself."

Replacing her bonnet, Julia moved to the door and, with a last concerned glance, slipped out of the chambers. Once alone, Kate flopped back onto the sofa and heaved a heavy sigh.

Blast. Blast. Blast.

What the devil was she to do?

What the devil was she up to?

Pacing the empty hallway, Luce glared at the stubbornly closed door to Kate's chambers. Only the fact that he had engaged her in a relentless inquisition assured him that the stubborn maiden was still within. As she had been for the entire day. Now, as the afternoon sun trailed steadily across the sky, he progressed from frustrated to downright concerned.

Why would she remain the entire day locked in her tiny chambers?

Was she ill? Was she troubled? Was she angry? Was she . . .

A dozen explanations, each more horrid than the last, raced through his mind. It was near the hour for tea when enough at last became enough.

Squaring his shoulders, Luce stepped across the hall and, without so much as a knock, thrust the door open. Rather to his surprise, it was unbolted and swung open easily. A swift glance revealed Kate curled on the sofa with her head laid back on the cushions.

"Kate." With a frown, he swiftly crossed the room to kneel beside the sofa. "What is it? Are you ill?"

With a blink, Kate slowly opened her eyes, as if she were just awakening from a nap.

"Luce?"

He reached to grasp her fingers. "Are you well?"

"Yes, of course." She gave a faint shake of her head, her gaze narrowing. "What are you doing here?"

"I was concerned. You have not left your chambers the entire day."

She scooted upright, her hands lifting to push back the burnished curls. "And how would you know that, Luce? Have you been watching my door?"

He smiled wryly. "Yes."

She blinked at his blunt honesty. "Why?"

"Because I am concerned for you." He regarded her darkened eyes with a faint frown. "Especially at this moment. Tell me why you have secluded yourself in these rooms. You have been dashing about London like a madwoman since you arrived. Something must have occurred to make you remain here the entire day."

Her lips thinned, and for a moment, he thought she might refuse to answer. Then, as if sensing he was not about to leave until he had a satisfactory explanation, she heaved a deep sigh.

"It is my father."

"Sir Frazer? Has he discovered your whereabouts?" he asked with a sharp stab of unease. An odd reaction, considering that the arrival of the older gentleman could only enhance his pressure upon Kate to become his wife. But then, he had already realized that he did not desire to force her to become his wife. When she walked down the aisle, it would be of her own will.

"No, but he is in London," she confessed in dark tones. "Along with an entire legion of my family. Julia arrived this morning to warn me."

"In London." He grimaced at the thought of encountering the puffed-up poppycock. "That is a rather unfortunate coincidence."

"Yes, you could say that," she retorted dryly.

"And so you are reduced to hiding in these rooms until he departs?"

She gave a restless shrug. "It is that or returning to Kent. I cannot risk being discovered."

Luce slowly levered himself to his feet, considering her dilemma. On one hand, there was a certain relief in having the unpredictable chit safely ensconced in her chambers. At least here she was in no danger of creating a scandal. Or worse, being in the company of that persistent cur, Lord Thorpe.

But, on the other hand, he possessed enough sense to realize that she would soon be frustrated and infuriated by her confinement. She would be pacing the floors and not at all in the humor to be wooed by even the most determined suitor.

Clearly something would have to be done.

And done swiftly.

Turning on his heel, Luce paced toward the shuttered window. He had taught himself over the years that there was never a problem that did not possess a solution. It was all a matter of sifting through every possibility. No matter how far-fetched the possibility.

Aware of Kate's gaze trained upon him with a wary puzzlement, Luce turned his concentration upon the various options. Startlingly the answer came with swift ease. Indeed, it was almost as if the thought had already been hiding in the back of his mind just awaiting the moment to make its appearance.

"Actually, there is another solution," he murmured as he turned to meet her narrowed gaze.

"Another solution? What do you mean?"

He hesitated, all too aware that whatever he might suggest, there was bound to be an argument. At the moment, Kate was so determined to maintain her fleeting independence that she would dig in her heels at even the most brilliant of notions.

At least if it came from him.

"Do you trust me, Kate?" he abruptly demanded.

She blinked, her lips parting as she struggled with her reply. "Trust you?"

He slowly crossed back toward the sofa, his gaze steadily holding her own. "It is a simple question, my dear."

"I . . . I do not know," she at last retorted.

Luce smiled wryly. Hardly an overwhelming display of confidence.

"Will you trust in me enough to discover the means of rescuing you from your current quandary?"

She wet her lips. "What do you intend to do?"

"I have a few thoughts in mind, but they all depend upon whether you will put yourself in my hands."

There was a long silence as she battled within herself. Clearly, she still considered him a blatant danger. And one that she would prefer to avoid.

Perhaps even to the point of risking her father's fury.

But even as he discovered himself smothering his painful wrench of disappointment, she seemed to come to a decision as she abruptly squared her shoulders.

"What do I need to do?"

Ridiculously, Luce felt his breath rushing from his lungs. As if he had just received a rare and utterly precious gift.

Squashing the urge to give a shout of triumph, he forced himself to maintain an air of brisk efficiency.

"You need do nothing more than pack a bag and inform the manager that you will be leaving London for a few days. I will take care of everything else."

"Luce . . ." She wavered, her teeth anxiously worrying her bottom lip. "I am not certain if I . . . if we . . ."

"Be at ease, Kate," he soothed. "I intend nothing more nefarious than keeping you hidden for the next few days. Once your father has returned to Kent, you can continue your pursuit of pleasure and adventure." He gave a brief bow as he headed firmly toward the door. Another few moments and she would convince herself she had just made a deal with the devil. "Be prepared early. I shall collect you before eight."

Not giving her the opportunity to debate his command, he slipped out the door and closed it behind him. Only then did he smile wryly at his absurd sense of satisfaction.

He might have momentarily managed to outmaneuver Miss Kate Frazer, but he could not fool himself that it was anything more than a brief aberration. One that would no doubt pass all too swiftly.

Oddly enough, however, his smile remained as he strolled with light steps down the hall.

Luce smiled with indulgent amusement at the unmistakable sound of Kate's shriek as it filled the air. Even above the chatter, whistles, and shouts from the crowd, he knew it was his delightful fiancée.

Pressing his way through the spectators that encircled the racetrack, he determinedly made his way to her side.

He suspected Kate would enjoy the thrilling excitement of the horse races. It was tailor-made for a woman seeking new experiences. Which was only one of the reasons he had chosen Brighton as their destination when they entered his rented carriage yesterday morning.

Unlike London, the resort town was nearly deserted of society, with only local gentry and wealthy merchants to take advantage of the various entertainments. They could easily mingle among the crowds with no concern of being recognized.

Still, for all of his confidence that Brighton would be the perfect location to hide Kate until her father's return to Kent, he had not been at all certain of her response.

She had been wary and on edge during the nearly six-hour carriage ride, and more than once, he had feared she might abruptly insist that she be returned to London. There had been another moment of tension when they arrived at the Castle Inn, where he checked them in as Mr. and Mrs. Freemont.

It was not until they had been led upstairs and she realized that he had requested two separate suites, albeit with a connecting door, that she seemed to accept he had not plotted to manipulate her into his bed.

Or worse, to the nearest vicar.

Confident that he seemed to mean no harm, Kate had arrived at breakfast this morning in surprisingly high spirits. She had questioned him

ceaselessly on the various entertainments and sights
that were to be discovered, clearly determined to
take advantage of her brief stay. And anxious to
prove he was more than capable of providing her
with all the adventure that she could possibly desire, Luce had swept her from the hotel to
promenade along the Steyne at the fashionable
hour of nine o'clock, followed by a visit to the growing monstrosity of Prinny's Marine Pavilion and
then to the seaside where one or two brave souls
dared the chilled beach.

After a light luncheon, he had been struck by in-
spiration and escorted her to the nearby races. And
he had not been disappointed in her enthusiastic
response.

With delightful abandon, she had thrown herself
into the hectic excitement that tingled in the air, although she had refused to allow him to place a
wager over a quid. Her insistence had made him
smile, knowing that it revealed a great deal of the
more conservative side, which she was determined
to ignore.

Her lack of extravagance in betting, however, did
not lessen her enthusiasm as she stood at the railing and loudly cheered her horse onward. Nor
dampen her excitement when one of her nags at
last crossed the finish line in first.

As Luce stood in a position to keep a close eye
upon her slender form, her happy shrieks called to
him like a siren's song.

Catching the flash of her titian curls in the pale
winter sunlight, Luce experienced an odd rush of
warmth. How could he not enjoy being with Kate?

She was so eager, so ready to embrace life that it
was impossible not to be infected. He felt younger
than he had in years. Perhaps since the day he had

realized his father's incessant folly and the weight of the world had been planted upon his shoulders. And for once, Kent and all those who depended upon him seemed far away.

Coming to a halt beside Kate, he allowed his gaze to slowly trail over her animated features. Lifting her head, she smiled deep into his eyes, making his heart do a most peculiar flop in his chest.

"Luce, did you see? Starlight came in first."

"So he did," he agreed, taking the slip of paper from her fingers before it was crumpled beyond repair. "Your luck seems to be in."

"Yes, indeed. I have never won upon a bet."

"A veritable fortune, indeed," he agreed dryly, realizing that she would barely come out a few pence ahead.

She wrinkled her nose in a charming manner. "Very well, you need not be so superior. I am well aware that I have lost far more than I have won."

"If you are aware of such a tedious calculation, then you are no true gambler," he murmured.

"Perhaps not." Her eyes flashed with an enticing glitter. "Still, it has been most enjoyable. And exciting. Far more exciting than I expected."

"You have never been to a racetrack before?" he asked softly.

"Good heavens, no. My father would not even allow me to attend the races during the local fair." She grimaced at the memory. "He claimed that such a boisterous entertainment was unseemly for maidens and, worse, inflamed the blood of young gentleman so that they could not be trusted to mind themselves as they should."

He regarded her delicate profile for a long moment. "Sir Frazer seemed to disapprove of a great many things. Especially those things that might bring a measure of happiness to his daughter."

The glitter in her eyes briefly dimmed. "I suppose he thought he was protecting me."

"There is a difference between wishing to protect someone and deliberately crushing them beneath one's will," he retorted in unwittingly disapproving tones.

"Not to my father's mind."

"Fah. He is fortunate that you did not rebel years ago."

Her lips twisted, although there was little amusement in her smile.

"There was not much danger of that," she retorted dryly. "As long as I can remember, I was far too anxious to prove I was the perfect daughter to offer any protest."

His chest seemed to tighten as he thought of her desperately attempting to please a father who would never acknowledge she was good enough. The thought was enough to make him want to hit something.

Preferably the florid countenance of Sir Frazer.

"No one is perfect," he said softly, gazing deep into her beautiful eyes. "Thank heavens. The world would be a dismal place without a few interesting flaws within all of us."

"Indeed?" Her earlier mood of infectious enjoyment returned as she gave a lift of her brow. "And what flaws will you confess to, my lord?"

He pretended to give great consideration to her teasing question. "Well, I must admit that I dislike vegetables, and I have been known to prefer the companionship of sailors and smugglers to that of polite society."

"And?" she prompted, not at all impressed with his confessions.

"I cannot carry a tune. In truth, I sound like a wounded hound whenever I attempt to sing."

"And?"

"And I possess a fear of bats."

She blinked. "Bats?"

"Nasty, dirty beasts who are forever hiding in the dark."

"Mmm . . ." She regarded him with a determined patience. "And that is the full list of your flaws? Vegetables, bats, and smugglers?"

Well aware of where she was leading, Luce allowed his lips to curve in a boyish smile. "For the most part, although I suppose there could be a rare few who might, just might, consider me the tiniest bit assertive when the occasion demands."

Kate gave a loud snort at his modest words. "A bit assertive? You are utterly arrogant and run roughshod over others without the least hint of remorse."

His smile faded as he reached out to lightly touch her soft cheek. "That is not entirely true, my dear. I have taken great care not to run roughshod over you, despite the very pressing temptation. Indeed, I believe it could be argued that I have allowed myself to be readily led upon your leash."

She blinked at his low words. "You upon a leash? Absurd."

He raised his brow. "Is it?"

For a moment she met his steady gaze, and then as if she were suddenly discomforted by the thought of possessing such a hold over him, she lowered her eyes.

"Of course."

Smiling wryly, he stepped closer to isolate them

from the milling crowd. "I have now admitted my flaws. It seems only fair that you offer a list of your own."

"Perhaps I have none," she murmured in low tones.

"Ah no, my dear, fair play demands that you reveal at least a few imperfections."

Her gaze slowly lifted, a reluctant smile tugging at her lovely lips. "Very well. I do have rather a sweet tooth and I have more than once slipped into the kitchen to filch an apple tart."

"For shame, Kate. A pastry thief?"

"Upon occasion." She gave a faint shrug.

"What else?"

"I fear I possess few talents. I dislike embroidery and painting and brought my pianoforte instructor to actual tears."

He pressed a hand to his heart in teasing shock. "A Philistine."

"And . . ."

"What?"

At his soft prompting, she heaved a sudden sigh. "And I have never been capable of following the Greek philosophy of moderation. It was never enough to be a good daughter—I had to be without fault. I could not give to charity to help the children—I had to create an orphanage. I could not merely claim my independence—I needed to run away from home and indulge in a scandalous charade."

Luce gave a slow shake of his head. "Such determination is not a flaw, my dear. It reveals a strength of character that I greatly admire."

A flush of color stained her cheeks at the husky sincerity in his voice. "I should think you would find it a source of annoyance."

"Why ever would you say that?"

"Obviously, if I were not quite so stubborn, I would still be in Kent and we should now be wed. Unless you have concluded that you would do better to choose another?"

A sharp, vivid image of this woman comfortably settled in his parlor, perhaps even perched upon his lap as they warmed themselves before the fire, became branded upon his mind. He was shocked by just how right it seemed. As if it had always been there, simply awaiting the proper woman to make it complete.

Within the image, Kate's expression was one of deep contentment.

Unfortunately, something decidedly absent at the moment.

"No, Kate, there will be no other," he said softly, his fingers cupping her cheek. "We belong together. Today and forever."

Her eyes flashed with something that might almost have been fear before she abruptly put a measure of space between them.

"I think the next race is getting ready to begin."

Luce suppressed a surge of impatience. Bloody hell. He considered himself a patient man. And one who understood maintaining a consistent strategy.

At the moment, however, the strategy of bundling her onto his ship and simply sailing away held infinite appeal.

"Do you wish to make another bet?" he forced himself to respond in mild tones.

She readily gave a shake of her head. "Oh no, I am quitting while I am winning. Or at least while I am not losing quite so badly."

"A wise choice," he murmured, casually taking her arm.

With a minimum of fuss, he collected the winnings, and handing Kate her bounty, he led her to the black carriage he had rented for the next week.

Once settled in the luxurious interior, Kate gave a pleased sigh and turned her head to regard him with an open curiosity.

"Where are we going?"

"It is a surprise," he informed her, lifting a hand to lazily play with a wayward curl that had fallen against her cheek. He felt a stab of satisfaction that she made no move to pull from his touch.

"You are suddenly fond of surprises," she murmured.

"Just one of my numerous charms."

"Oh." She gave a lift of her brow. "You possess more than one charm?"

"I possess an endless fund, I assure you." He leaned closer, a wicked glow in his eyes. "Of course, a demonstration of my more potent charms will have to wait until later."

He thought her breath might have caught at his insinuating words, but her gaze never strayed from his face.

"What are you doing here, Luce?"

The soft question came without warning, and Luce instinctively retreated behind a casual smile.

"What do you imagine I am doing? Enjoying the delights of Brighton with a beautiful and enticing young maiden."

Of course, Kate had proved she was not to be easily swayed by sweet words and a boyish grin. Now she merely narrowed her gaze.

"Surely you are needed in Kent? What of your family?"

He shrugged. "They are capable of surviving a few weeks without me."

"And what of the fortune you must have?" she demanded with indisputable logic. "Surely you should be seeking another wife?"

"Perhaps I have decided to follow in your footsteps to enjoy today and allow tomorrow to take care of itself."

"Balderdash." She gave a disbelieving laugh, no doubt well aware his fierce sense of responsibility would never allow him to disregard his pressing duties. "I would as soon believe that pigs could fly."

He arched his brows at her chiding words. "I am here, am I not?"

"Only because you have some purpose in mind," she said, her expression knowing. "I may be naive, but not so naive that I do not realize you could not have given up so easily. Not at the risk of seeing your family disgraced and your business ruined."

Luce's fingers absently stroked the satin cream of her cheek. It was true enough. He would not allow his family or his business to be harmed. No matter what the sacrifice.

Still, seated alone with this titian-haired sprite, his thoughts were not upon his family or business.

"At the moment, my only interest is in you," he said in husky tones. "And ensuring your pleasure. Whatever that pleasure might be."

Her eyes darkened even as she struggled to remain impervious to the awareness prickling between them.

"You cannot put off the inevitable, Luce. You shall soon enough have to turn your attentions elsewhere."

No, he inwardly told himself.

His attentions would not be straying elsewhere. Not when they so clearly belonged together.

He was wise enough, however, not to set up her hackles. For the moment, she was determined to pretend she could ignore the future. And the realization that her only true hope of independence was marriage to him.

She would eventually come to her senses and he would patiently be waiting to whisk her home.

"All the more reason to enjoy myself while we are together, would you not agree?" he teased with a slow smile.

"I suppose that depends," she retorted warily.

"On what?"

"On how you intend to enjoy yourself."

He gave a soft chuckle. "Dinner first, and then . . . who knows what the night might hold?"

CHAPTER EIGHT

Magic.

There was simply no other word for the beauty that surrounded her.

Kate drew in a deep breath as she leaned against the stone railing of the terrace. The ancient castle had been built atop the highest bluff, with a wide terrace that offered a stunning view of the vast sea and frost-kissed sky. She felt bathed in the rosy glow and at complete peace with herself.

To think she might have missed all this, Kate thought with a sigh. Indeed, until the very moment she had allowed Luce to place her in his carriage and drive away from the hotel, she had continued to warn herself she was making a dangerous mistake.

She was not a fool. She knew that he still thought to make her his bride.

But even as she sternly warned herself to return to her rooms and lock the door, she had stepped into the carriage and allowed herself to be whisked away.

And why should she not? she had argued with the voice of sense. She had precious little time left before she would have to return to Kent. It would surely be a waste to choose days locked in her chambers when she could be out enjoying adventures.

And if Luce could provide the adventure . . .

well, that certainly did not mean she had to marry the man.

Hearing the soft approach of footsteps, Kate allowed a smile to curve her lips. Whatever her concerns, she could not deny that he was a master of creating a wonderful adventure. What other gentleman would have thought to arrange an elegant picnic within the picturesque ruins?

"You have become very pensive. What are you thinking?" he demanded, turning to lean against the railing so that he was facing her rather than the beauty below.

"I was just appreciating the view," she admitted.

He arched a golden brow, his features oddly softened in the growing darkness.

"It is certainly more pleasant than London. No traffic, no choking air, no unfortunate relatives."

She gave a slow smile. "You dislike London?"

"It is a necessary evil that I endure for the sake of my business, but I will admit a preference for the country."

"And what of the sea?"

"It was once my haven," he said in soft tones. "But one that is no longer necessary. Now I long for a quiet life surrounded by my family." His lips twisted in a wry smile. "A dull dream for you, my dear, but one that I have never had the pleasure of experiencing. I find myself longing for quiet nights settled by the fire with you in my arms and your sweet scent filling the room."

Kate unconsciously frowned, her fingers tight upon the railing. It was terrifyingly easy to imagine such a domestic scene. And worse, to imagine herself warmly snuggled next to his steady strength with no desire to ever leave.

"What of your business?" she demanded, in an

effort to distract her renegade thoughts. "Surely you cannot simply abandon it?"

He lifted a negligent shoulder. "I will, of course, always maintain control of my business, but for now it is the estate that is in need of my most strenuous efforts. Especially considering my lack of knowledge of how best to be a good landlord. It will take time to discover all I need to know as Earl of Calfield." He paused for a moment before continuing in low tones. "And the assistance of a devoted wife."

Wife.

A shiver inched down her spine as she threatened to become lost in the warmth of his steady gaze.

With a deliberate effort to shake off his oddly hypnotic spell, she forced a smile to her stiff lips.

"So you intend to trade in your position as a pirate for that of a farmer?" she questioned in light tones. "You should make an interesting addition to the local assemblies and soirees."

Readily following her lead to lighten the mood, he reached up to give a gentle tug on a wayward curl. "Brat. I will have you know that not all sailors are by profession pirates."

She raised a brow in teasing disbelief. "No, only the successful ones."

His lips twitched. "Well, at least I have always been the most civilized of pirates. And I do not think I shall terrorize the neighborhood too greatly."

No. He would not terrorize the neighborhood, she wryly acknowledged, but he would most certainly stir it to a fever pitch. Unwittingly, she let her gaze travel over the lean form attired in a black coat and dove gray breeches. What woman in her senses would not secretly weave fantasies about the delicious earl, even in his casual country attire ? And what gentleman would not seek to ape his elegant style and commanding air?

There was a vibrant energy about him that spoke of power and a ruthless determination that would draw attention like a bee to nectar.

"A civilized pirate?" she lightly retorted. "Is that not rather like an honest thief?"

"Very well, my wench." Without warning, his arms reached out to encircle her waist and he pulled her against his hard body. Sparks seemed to fly as their forms collided and he smiled deeply into her wide eyes. "If I am a pirate that means you are my bounty. Now, *that* I like very much."

Kate discovered that she liked it very much as well.

She liked the heat that surrounded her. The scent of his male skin. The feel of his hands spread across her lower back. The sharp dart of anticipation that arrowed straight to the pit of her stomach.

And the deep sense of sanctuary she felt in his arms.

As if she had found the only place she truly belonged.

A sudden chill inched down her spine and it was only with an effort she maintained her impression of bantering ease.

"Ah, but you are determined to become a farmer, and no longer be a pirate, my lord," she retorted, although her voice was revealingly breathless. "And I assure you that farmers do not behave in such a manner."

His hands tightened on her back, a sudden color staining his high cheekbones. "Considering the fact that any number of farmers are readily producing an entire flock of heirs, I find your logic rather flawed, my sweet. Indeed, I would guess that they behave in such a manner on a regular basis."

A rash of prickles raced over her skin.

"Luce, do not," she muttered.

Ignoring her weak protest, he dropped his gaze to the softness of her mouth.

"Dear God, I ache to kiss you."

Feeling oddly breathless, Kate struggled not to melt into a puddle at his feet.

"Luce, I will not be seduced into marriage."

He growled deep in his throat. "Stop it, Kate. This has nothing to do with marriage, or dowries, or empty coffers." His gaze stabbed her with its glittering force. "This is nothing more than a man who is desperate to taste of a woman's sweetness."

Kate felt his fingers tremble as they pressed into her back, and she blinked at the unexpected sense of satisfaction that filled her.

Luce did want her, she acknowledged with a sense of wonder. Beyond his cunning plans to lure her back to Kent. Beyond his need for wealth.

There was no mistaking the taut lines of his body. The rasp of his breath and the restless hunger in his eyes.

A strange sensation rushed through her and Kate caught her breath. She had never before experienced the feeling of being truly desired.

It was dangerously enticing.

Too enticing.

"Luce, you must release me."

"Why?" His breath brushed her heated skin. "Do you find my touch revolting? Does it not please you?"

A cowardly part of her longed to agree. To tell him that she did indeed find his touch revolting. Such a confession would no doubt put a swift end to this wicked encounter, and perhaps even to his determined pursuit.

Unfortunately, she feared her body was already revealing the unmistakable truth. He could not fail to notice the thunder of her heart or the faint tremors of pleasure she could not hide.

"You know I do not, but . . . it is not proper."

He gave a soft chuckle at her ridiculous words. "I thought that you had left behind being proper in Kent? Are you not the maiden who is determined to seek all sorts of adventures? To taste of life and all it might offer?"

He was right, blast his arrogance. This was precisely what she had dreamed of when she had fled Kent. A glorious flirtation with a handsome rake.

When she had been in Kent, however, passion and need had been no more than the stuff of romantic poets. It not had been a tangible, sharp-edged ache that threatened her very senses.

"It grows late," she muttered in uneven tones. "We should return soon."

A sigh rushed through his lips as he placed his forehead against hers. "Someday you will trust me, Kate. Someday soon."

She stiffened at the implication that she would concede defeat. As if she would be swayed by the pleasure of his touch.

"You are very confident in your skills, my lord."

"No, not confident. Just accepting of a fate you insist upon fighting," he corrected, shifting to brush his lips over her brow. "Now, as you said, it grows late."

Her heart halted at the soft caress, before galloping back into motion as if to make up for lost time.

"Yes," she murmured, awkwardly stepping backward.

Gads, she felt as if she had been tossed into a stormy sea with no idea if she would sink or swim.

* * *

Luce watched the stone he had tossed sink into the sea.

It was a wretched morning for a stroll. A chilled fog thickened the air, reminding the unwary that winter was indeed here. Still, it was preferable to pacing the cramped rooms at the inn.

As was becoming all too familiar, he had awoken well before dawn after a near sleepless night. A damnable predicament for a gentleman who had managed to rest even when sailing upon the stormiest waters.

Gads, not even the past two days of escorting his seemingly inexhaustible companion from one entertainment to another had managed to mute the restless impatience that coursed through his blood.

A wry smile abruptly touched his lips. Bloody hell. Of course, being with Miss Kate Frazer had not eased his restlessness. This burning in his blood was entirely due to the frustrating minx.

He had been a fool.

He had known before bringing her to Brighton that he desired her. No, that he increasingly ached for her sweetness. And that being in her constant company was bound to be a form of masculine torture.

But while he had prepared himself for the pangs of physical need, and battling temptation, he had somehow failed to consider the power of simply having her near.

Reaching down, Luce collected another hapless pebble and jerkily tossed it into the waves.

How could he not be enchanted by her vibrant spirit and startling wit? Or by her unexpected displays of kindness toward all those about her?

She was a rare woman, made all the more rare by

the sheer courage that had allowed her to maintain even a measure of herself beneath her father's grim rule.

With every passing moment, he became more certain that she was created to be his wife.

And yet, for all his certainty, she remained determinedly elusive. Oh, he sensed that she was attracted to him. And that she enjoyed his companionship. There were even moments when he would swear that she felt the relentless bond between them as fiercely as he did.

But for every step he took toward her, she managed to slip two back. A frustrating waltz that threatened to drive him batty.

Luce shivered as another gust of wind tugged at his caped greatcoat, then slowly he stilled in awareness. Although the enticing scent was faint he would know it in his sleep.

Turning about, he discovered Kate standing a few paces away, her slender form enveloped in a cherry red cloak with black fur about the hood. His chest seemed to tighten even as he carefully smoothed his features to a casual expression.

"Good morning, my sweet," he murmured, moving to face her. "You are up and about earlier than usual on this rather dismal day."

She wrinkled her slender nose as she glanced at the fog-shrouded sky. "Remaining beneath my warm covers was certainly a temptation, but then I realized that I mustn't allow myself to waste a moment in Brighton. We will, after all, have to return to London quite soon."

Luce allowed his gaze to sweep over the purity of her alabaster features. She appeared unexpectedly fragile wrapped in the heavy velvet, her cheeks flushed with cold.

"There is no hurry," he murmured, not at all anxious to return Kate to London and the endless distractions it provided. "We are at liberty to remain as long as you desire."

Her eyes briefly darkened as she gave a shake of her head. "No, we cannot remain. My father no doubt has already returned to Kent. It would be best to leave on the morrow."

"There is something, or perhaps someone, awaiting you in London?" he demanded, regretting the unmistakably possessive words as soon as they tumbled from his lips.

As expected, she swiftly took a defensive step back, her expression guarded. "I believe I shall take a short stroll before breakfast. Perhaps I will see you when I return."

Silently cursing his stupidity, he firmly took her arm and entwined it with his own. "Oh no. You are not getting rid of me so easily. Where shall we stroll? The Steyne? Or would you prefer to view the Pavilion?"

Standing so close, he could feel her slightly stiffen at his insistence, but thankfully, she did not pull away.

"Actually, the chamber maid was telling me this morning of an ancient legend I hoped to investigate."

"Ancient legend?" He lifted his golden brows as he tilted his head to one side. "What sort of legend?"

"The legend of the Mad Monk and his hidden treasure."

Luce gave a sudden laugh at her startling childish desire to hunt for hidden treasure.

"Odd. I would hardly think that a monk would have much of a treasure."

She offered a small smile. "Well, it is rumored

that he was traveling to a monastery in France, but that along the way to London, he fell violently in love with a village maiden," she explained in soft tones. "Unfortunately, her parents refused to countenance a match with an impoverished wanderer. Especially after they had already received a large promise of wealth from a prosperous merchant who desired her. In the end, he left to make his fortune upon the seas as a pirate."

His lids lowered slightly as he audaciously reached out to brush a stray curl away from her cheek.

"Please do not disappoint me and say that while he was gone, she treacherously gave into the wiles of the merchant, and the poor distraught monk tossed himself and his treasure into the sea."

"No, indeed. His beloved remained true, but the day before he arrived, she died while giving birth to his child. In his grief, the monk decided to punish the greedy parents in the most devious manner. He buried his massive treasure somewhere near their home and then simply disappeared."

"Ah, quite a cruel revenge, indeed." He smiled gently as his fingers brushed down to the line of her jaw. He could understand how the romantic tale had caught her fancy. "It must have driven them mad to know that there was a fortune within their grasp and yet be unable to discover its location."

"It is said that their ghosts still roam the cliffs in search of the treasure."

"Of course. What is a good treasure hunt without ghosts?" He paused a moment, regarding her fragile beauty. "Are you certain you shall be warm enough? The breeze is quite chill."

She gave a small shrug. "I am rarely affected by the weather. But I would not have you suffer for my folly. I will quite understand if you prefer to remain at the inn."

Luce felt a sharp pang. When he first met Kate, he had presumed that he could read her like an open book. There was no artifice, no cunning that he too often found in others. Now he discovered that he had not the faintest notion what she was thinking.

If she desired his companionship or wished him in the netherworld.

It was not at all a comfortable sensation.

"I will come," he said firmly. "I cannot allow you to wander off in the fog with dangerous ghosts and mad monks on the loose."

"You need have no fear, Luce. I have it on excellent authority that they only make their appearance during a full moon."

He smiled wryly. "And what of other unscrupulous rascals that might be lurking just out of sight?"

Her brows pulled together. "Good heavens, Luce, I am perfectly capable of taking care of myself. I have no need for a guardian at my age."

A startling flare of anger shuddered through him before Luce forced himself to take a calming breath.

Blast, there were moments when this woman could test the patience of a saint.

Why did she continue to thrust him away? Why would she not admit that they could possess something wondrous? Something that could endure for the rest of their lives.

Why? Why? Why?

Thoroughly disgruntled, Luce realized that Kate was regarding him with an expectant gaze. With an effort, he managed a stiff smile.

"No. Where you go, I go, Kate."

"But . . ."

His hands reached out to frame her face. "You are not going anywhere without me. We are in this together."

CHAPTER NINE

Not allowing herself the opportunity for second thoughts, Kate turned away from the disturbing gentleman at her side to walk toward the narrow path leading to the distant cliffs.

Perhaps she should have been more insistent that she be allowed to enjoy her adventure alone, she acknowledged ruefully. No, not *perhaps*. *Definitely,* she should have been more insistent.

She had been well aware of the danger Luce posed since the moment he had arrived in London. A danger that had become even more perilous over the past few days.

How often since arriving in Brighton had she allowed herself to forget that Luce was only with her for her dowry? How often had she caught herself covertly studying his handsome countenance and magnificent form? How often had they laughed together as if they were truly friends?

How often had she longed to lean forward and press her lips to his?

He was not the man she had thought him to be. Certainly he could be arrogant and commanding, but he was also kind and thoughtful and startlingly tender.

Precisely the sort of gentleman any maiden would be in danger of tumbling irrevocably in love with.

It was that realization that had belatedly prompted her determination to return to London. She had to put an end to her time with Luce, she had warned herself when she awoke this morning. And she had to put an end to it today.

But even as the decision was being made, she had felt her resolve faltering.

They had one day and one night left until they returned to London. One day and one night they were virtually trapped with each other.

What could possibly be the harm in waiting one more day to bring an end to their tenuous camaraderie? a renegade voice had whispered.

Just a handful of hours before she informed Luce she was moving on to a new adventure.

And so, perhaps cowardly, she kept her thoughts to herself as they slowly forged their way through the fog and up the steep path leading to the bluff.

She was uncertain why she had been attracted to the chilling tale the chambermaid had revealed this morning. Surely every village and town in England possessed a ghost story? Perhaps it was the excitement of a buried treasure. Or of briefly reliving the past.

Or, more likely, she merely felt a measure of connection with the poor maiden being crushed under the relentless will of her parents and unable to seek the happiness she desired.

Whatever the cause, she knew that she wanted to walk the bluff at least once before leaving for London.

Glancing to the side, she silently studied Luce's proud, elegant profile. He had spoken very little and she knew that he had been annoyed by her insistence upon returning to London. Perhaps he was even considering the wisdom of turning his attentions to a less stubborn heiress.

The thought brought an unexpected pang, and she hurriedly sought to distract her unwelcome broodings.

"I suppose that within an estate as old as Calfield Park you must possess a ghost or two," she murmured.

He turned to regard her with a smoldering gaze before his features slowly softened with a rueful smile.

"Most certainly not," he retorted as he carefully skirted her past a fallen log. "We may harbor rakes, scoundrels, and on occasion, dastards, but the Calfields have never been troubled by bothersome ghosts."

She lifted her brows at his deliberately arrogant manner. "You believe your family above a good haunting?"

"Above? No. Well, at least not precisely. It is more a matter of possessing the proper ancestors."

"You mean ancestors who are gracious enough to remain politely in their graves?"

The breeze ruffled his golden hair as he bent his head toward her. "No, I mean ancestors who were not entirely human."

"What?"

He gave a chuckle at her shocked expression. "You have not heard of the very first Calfield, who fell in love with a mermaid?"

In spite of her turbulent emotions, Kate discovered herself intrigued. The Frazers had always been a prodigiously dull lot throughout the centuries without so much as a highwayman or daring rascal, let alone an enchanted creature.

Now she slowed her pace to regard him with unmistakable curiosity. "Do you mean to say that you possess the blood of a mermaid?"

"So the story goes," he confessed with a smile. "My distant grandfather was foolish enough to become entrapped in the mermaid's bewitchment, and he refused to leave his watery paradise until she had given him a child to take as a memento."

"A most sentimental gentleman," she murmured.

"Thank goodness the mermaid was of the same opinion," he teased. "Rather than cursing him to some horrid fate, which is the usual case with such capricious creatures, she blessed him with a son and a beautiful glade to raise him in. If you visit Calfield Park, you will discover mermaids gracing the conservatory as well as painted on several ceilings, in her honor." His smile widened. "Even my bed is engraved with mermaids, if you desire a private viewing."

Her heart performed its familiar leap as she regarded his utterly male countenance. In the misty fog there was something different about him. He appeared more the pirate she had claimed him rather than a proper gentleman, and a tingle of renegade excitement flared through her body at the indecently bold shimmer within the dark blue eyes and the reckless, dangerous beauty about him.

"A most charming invitation, but I fear I must decline," she forced herself to murmur.

"A pity."

It was a pity, she thought. She did not doubt that he would prove to be a most glorious seducer. One who would ensure a woman was well-pleased in his arms. A shiver raced through her before she was firmly scrubbing such treacherous emotions away.

"You still have not revealed why Calfield Park has no ghosts."

His gaze swept over her flushed countenance in a slow, lingering manner. "Because it is enchanted, of course. No spirits or monsters or evil demons are allowed in the glade. It was the mermaid's spell to protect her lover and son. Supposedly we are even protected from fire, although we have always been wise enough not to place our trust in a fading legend and take all the necessary precautions as other estates."

She smiled faintly. "Perhaps it is your mermaid blood that makes you so fond of the sea."

"Certainly," he readily agreed, a wicked amusement entering his eyes. "And, of course, it also accounts for my astonishing charm and beauty."

"Fah. Now I know you are only jesting. I—" Kate's words came to an abrupt end as she glanced toward the nearby bluff.

Swiftly on alert, Luce regarded her with a frown. "What is it, Kate?"

"I thought I heard a noise. Almost a . . . cry."

"No doubt a seagull, but I should make sure." He sent her a stern glance. "I want you to wait here."

"But . . ."

"I will be only a moment." Waiting for her to give a reluctant nod, Luce brushed his lips casually over her forehead before striding through the fog toward the edge of the bluff.

For a moment he merely stood there, and Kate ruefully cursed herself for allowing thoughts of ghosts and mermaids to have set her nerves on edge. Then, turning about, Luce waved her toward him with an odd expression.

Crossing the short distance, she halted at his side. "What is it?"

"It appears we have a small companion to assist us in enjoying the fine view."

She frowned in puzzlement at his smooth words. "A companion?"

Covertly, his hand moved to point over the edge of the cliff. "Yes, indeed. A most charming chap named Billie, although he is somewhat occupied at the moment with studying the beauty of nature."

Warily, Kate peeked over the edge. What she saw made her heart jump to her throat.

"Dear heavens," she breathed in horror, regarding the tiny, freckle-faced boy who was grimly clinging to a small ledge. At the same moment, she felt a touch upon her arm, and she glanced up to discover Luce giving a faint shake of his head. Abruptly, she realized that he was warning her not to frighten the child into making any sudden moves. With an effort, she swallowed her fear and offered the boy a small smile. "What a very peculiar spot to choose to linger. Are you pretending to be a seagull?"

"No, Miss." The lad bravely blinked back the tears that threatened. "I . . . I was thinking to search for the pirate treasure."

Kate bit her lip, belatedly realizing that foolishly romantic maidens would not be the only ones lured to seeking the Mad Monk's fortune.

"I see. A very bold adventure, but it is nearly time for breakfast. Perhaps it would be best to continue your search another day?"

"I . . . I am cruelly hungry," he admitted even as he huddled more firmly upon the ledge. "But I think I might stay just a mite longer."

Realizing he was far too terrified to move on his own, Kate gave a nod of her head. "If you wish. Do you mind if I remain to keep you company?"

He offered a watery smile. "I should like that very much."

"Good." Keeping her attention upon the boy,

Kate knelt as Luce began to ease himself a short way down the cliff and then over the side. It was obvious that he hoped to rescue Billie while she kept him distracted. She leaned down further, well aware that it was imperative that the boy not sense Luce's approach. One wrong move and . . . she sucked in a steadying breath. "Do you know, I am out here to search for the hidden treasure as well?"

"You are?"

Her lips twitched at his obvious surprise. Clearly he thought her too old to be daring enough to search for a legendary booty.

"Oh yes. I believe it must be very wonderful to discover a chest filled with ribbons and bows and pretty gowns."

As expected, Billie grimaced in horrified disdain. "Cripes, that ain't no treasure."

"It isn't?"

"Course not. What would a pirate be wanting with bows and ribbons?"

Her breath caught as her sideways glance revealed that Luce was boldly moving over the jagged rocks toward the young boy. He seemed utterly unaware of the danger as he easily pulled himself toward the ledge.

She clenched her hands in fear as she returned her attention to her young friend.

"What do you suppose the treasure to be, Billie?"

He offered her a condescending sigh. "Why everyone knows it is gold coins and swords and diamonds as big as a meat pie."

"Good heavens, whatever would you do with such riches?"

He took a moment to consider the pleasure of uncovering such a bounty. Thankfully, he did not seem to note the sound of pebbles being dislodged just behind him.

"I should buy me ma a beautiful carriage so that she could drive about like a fancy lady, and me pa a new plow."

"Why, that is a lovely notion, Billie, but I believe your parents would be even more pleased to simply have you home with them."

His expression crumpled and the tears once again threatened. "Yes, Miss. I should dearly love to be home as well. Me ma promised to have muffins for tea."

Kate smiled in relief as the man moved onto the ledge and was within easy reach of the child.

"Muffins? Then, indeed, we must ensure you are returned home with all possible haste."

"But . . ." Billie's protest was abruptly halted and he let loose a shrill screech as Luce firmly grasped him about the waist and hoisted him upward.

Already suspecting what was about to occur, Kate was prepared to reach out and grasp the dangling form, wrapping him in her arms and pulling him away from the edge of the cliff. Once safe upon the grass, she continued to hold his shaking body close, pressing her cheek to his tousled hair.

"Here now, you are safe, Billie," she soothed, her anxious gaze remaining trained upon the edge of the cliff as Luce brazenly risked life and limb to pull himself upward and over the sharp precipice. Once again standing upon firm ground, he pushed back his ruffled golden hair as if he climbed about dangerous cliffs every day. "Nothing is going to happen to you."

Still shaking, the boy nevertheless managed to pull from her grasp and swat at the tears that had flowed freely down his grimy face.

"I wasn't frightened, Miss," he said in choked tones. "Not truly."

"No, of course not," she quickly agreed. "You are a very brave lad."

With a sniff, Billie's eyes abruptly widened as the sound of a distant voice calling his name echoed through the air.

"Ma. Oh lordy, she will be ever so mad I have been gone so long."

Kate reached out to ruffle his red hair. "You had best run along. Those muffins will not stay warm for long."

With a sudden smile, the lad was scurrying toward the nearby path, clearly recovering from his near disaster with a speed only a child could accomplish.

Kate watched his hurried retreat before slowly turning to regard Luce with warm admiration. He had been . . . spectacular. A hero who had charged to the rescue with as much courage and daring as any warrior from ancient stories.

Just at the point of revealing how much she admired what he had done, Kate suddenly widened her eyes, and she tilted back her head to laugh with rich enjoyment.

Luce scowled with fierce discomfort.

Bloody hell. This was not how a knight in shining armor was supposed to be treated. Good grief, he had saved a child, at some not inconsiderable risk to himself, and returned him to his terrified family. But rather than being greeted with kisses and rose petals that were only suitable for a knight of old, he had been laughed at, mocked, and followed back to the inn by giggling children.

It was all decidedly unjust.

Of course, he had to admit he did not appear particularly knightly at the moment. His lips twitched with irrepressible humor as he glanced down at his once elegant attire, now thickly coated with a layer of mud. If truth be told, he looked more like something that had been found in the bogs than a gentleman.

Glancing up, Luce met the twinkling gaze of Kate as she stood in the center of her chambers. Through the connecting door he could hear the servants preparing the hot bath he had ordered, but for the moment, he was unfortunately trapped in the rapidly drying muck.

"I suppose you find this amusing, my sweet?" he demanded with an expression of magnificent disgust.

"Of course not. You were very brave, Luce," she said in choked tones.

He lifted a brow at her patent lie. "Then why are you laughing?"

She struggled a moment before her treacherous laughter rang through the room. "I was just thinking of those children as they followed us back to the inn."

He planted his hands on his hips, flakes of dried mud fluttering to the carpet.

"You did precious little to halt their jesting."

Another bubble of laughter rose to her lips as she recalled the merry parade that had drawn the attention of every household in Brighton.

"Well, it is not every day that they are treated to the sight of a nobleman covered in mud. They thought you the true Mad Monk."

"No, just a Mad Nobleman," he protested. "Made all the more mad by allowing himself to be lured into traipsing through the fog and mud for a nonexistent treasure, I might add."

She gave a remarkably unsympathetic shrug. "I did tell you that you need not come with me."

His gaze narrowed as he gave a slow shake of his head. "And I told you that you are not going anywhere without me," he retorted in possessive tones. "Speaking of which, I believe my bath is almost prepared. Would you care to join me? We could share luncheon among the bubbles."

Not surprisingly, that ready blush touched her soft features. "Actually, I believe I would prefer to share luncheon without bubbles and with a gentleman who is not quite such an interesting shade of gray."

"My dear, I am wounded," he murmured, taking a step forward. "I was after all forced to endure humiliation after so heroically saving a young lad from his perch upon the cliff. Surely that is worthy of some reward?"

Her lips twitched at his words. "Are good works not supposed to be a reward in themselves?"

He allowed his gaze to sweep over her slender form, enticingly revealed by the soft peach gown.

"I prefer a more . . . tangible reward."

She seemed to catch her breath at his soft words before she was sternly meeting his wicked gaze.

"Perhaps Billie's mother would be willing to share her muffins. He seemed to believe they were quite tasty."

He wrinkled his nose. "Not at all what I had in mind."

"I fear that is the best offer you are going to receive," she pertly retorted.

A rueful amusement rippled over his mud-crusted features. "At least assure me that you were suitably impressed with my attempt to play the role of the knight in shining armor."

"Oh, I was definitely impressed," she assured him.

"Then I suppose being the town's temporary jester was not entirely a waste of a morning." He tilted his head to one side. "You are certain about that bath?"

She wrinkled her nose at the pungent layer of sticky mud. "Very sure."

"Then how about a kiss to sooth my bruised pride?"

"Umm . . . I believe I shall have to decline."

He heaved a disappointed sigh. "You are a hard and heartless woman, Miss Kate Frazer."

"No, I am a clean and tidy woman, and I intend to stay that way," she informed him with a smile. "However, if you must insist upon a reward for your heroic deeds, I will order a tea tray with your favorite apple tarts."

"Mmm . . . actually, I believe apple tarts are your favorite, Kate."

"Really? How very odd."

He gave a low chuckle before turning and heading into his chamber. Despite the trials of the morning, he felt strangely lighthearted. Well, perhaps not so strange.

Since his rescue of young Billie, there had been no mistaking the increased warmth within Kate. Oh, it had not been anything dramatic. She had not suddenly tossed herself at his feet. Or proclaimed the words of never-dying devotion he longed to hear. But there had been a definite thaw.

It had been in the manner in which she had regarded him with those fascinating, changeable eyes. In the manner in which she had reached out to touch him when they were returning from the cliffs. And in the manner in which her expression had softened when she gazed at him.

The wary barriers that she kept so rigidly between them were beginning to falter. Now he had
to make certain that they crumbled completely.
And he had to do so with enough finesse that he
did not inadvertently ruin what progress he had
managed to make.

A rather fine-edged sword.

With a wave of his hands, he dismissed the hovering servants and began peeling the stiffened
clothes from his body. Then, with a deep sigh, he
sank into the warm water and thankfully scrubbed
the filth from his hair and countenance.

A part of him longed to linger in the refreshing
warmth and simply soak away the chill that seemed
to have settled in his very bones from their lengthy
walk. But a larger part of him was far too impatient
to return to Kate's company to waste a moment.

They had only a few hours left in Brighton. He
had to ensure that she was truly his before they returned to London.

With that thought in mind, Luce left the bath
and attired himself in a dark blue coat and a silver
waistcoat studded with pearls. His golden hair was
still damp, but he combed the locks in an elegant
style toward his countenance and even took the tedious effort of tying his cravat into a far more
elaborate knot than usual.

At last deciding he had done all that was possible
to make the maiden's heart flutter, he gave a tug on
his cuffs and moved across the room to pull open
the connecting door.

Rather to his amazement, he experienced the
oddest flutter in the pit of his stomach. Nerves?
Surely not.

He had faced his father's drunken fury. Raging
seas. Murderous pirates.

How the devil could a slip of a girl rattle his fire-forged courage?

It was absurd.

Dragging in a deep breath, Luce forced himself forward, not halting until he had crossed the chamber and was settling his long form on the sofa next to the titian-haired beauty. Perhaps a strategic mistake, he ruefully acknowledged as her warmth and alluring scent wrapped about him.

His intent was to charm, not to pounce.

Although . . . no, no, no. Definitely no pouncing.

Fiercely gathering his frayed control, he met her searching gaze with a smile.

"Well, my dear, I do hope that you have ordered a lavish tea," he teased as he settled back in the cushions and draped an arm over the back of the sofa. "I have discovered that toting half the countryside back to the inn upon my clothing has given me rather a sharp appetite."

"Actually there was no need." She leaned forward to pull the cloth off a large tray set on the table before them. What she revealed was an astonishing feast with thin-sliced ham, stuffed mushrooms, braised potatoes, and strawberries in cream. "It seems that the inn's cook happens to be an aunt to young Billie and, after learning of your daring deeds, decided that you were in need of a reward."

"Good God." Luce regarded the platters with genuine surprise. "Did someone tell her that an entire battalion rescued Billie?"

Her lips twitched. "No, just one very muddy knight in shining armor."

"Ah, but now I am a well-scrubbed knight in shining armor," he pointed out as he reached for a strawberry.

"Yes, and decidedly less pungent."

He flashed her a scandalized glance. "Pungent? I will have you know that a Peer of the Realm is never pungent."

"Aromatic?"

"Fragrant."

"Fah." She wrinkled her nose at his teasing. "Your fragrance reeked to high heaven."

"Very well, I might have carried with me a . . . scent of muck and mire, but now I am freshly scrubbed." He allowed his hand to drift along the back of the sofa toward her bare neck. "Of course if you have doubt I could always return to the bath and you could ensure that I did not miss a . . ."

"That is quite all right," she firmly interrupted, although her eyes glittered with amusement rather than the wariness he had come to dread. And most shockingly, she did not even attempt to pull away from his light touch. "I will trust you managed to scrape off the worst."

He heaved a deep sigh. "And I thought being a knight in shining armor would mean at least a few favors from my favorite damsel."

"Favors?"

Of their own volition, his fingers cupped the back of her neck. Despite all his stern warnings not to press this maiden into full retreat, her flirtatious manner was impossible to resist.

He was a gentleman and a pirate, not a saint.

"It is tradition, you know."

"I . . ." She licked her full lips and Luce knew he was lost.

With a low groan, he slowly lowered his head to that tempting mouth. "Allow me to demonstrate, my sweet."

CHAPTER TEN

The hotel had not changed.

There was still a polite hush that clung to the cozy lobby, a lovely spice of freshly cut flowers in the soft air and the tempting scent of baking bread that escaped from the nearby kitchens.

Kate felt a shiver sneak down her spine as she climbed the wide stairs to her chambers.

She was uncertain what she had expected.

It had, after all, been only a few days since she left London. What could possibly have changed beyond the odd guest or two?

But Kate knew she had expected it to be different. Perhaps because she was different. The handful of days alone with Luce might have been an eternity.

She had left the city as a willful child who believed she possessed the will and the divine right to control her destiny. She had presumed herself in utter command of her fate.

Now she realized just how foolish she had been.

No one controlled fate, destiny, or . . . the treachery of a willful heart.

Not even the new, daring, utterly reckless Miss Kate Frazer.

Which only made it more imperative that she flee

from Lord Calfield, she acknowledged with a covert glance at the man walking silently at her side.

Her breath seemed to be caught in a relentless vise as she recalled how, earlier that morning, he had solicitously ensured that she was warm enough in the carriage and provided her with the apple tarts he had ordered from the kitchen. He had even commanded the driver to halt at a small cottage so that he could ease his mind that Billie had not experienced any ill effects from his adventure.

There had been a poignant sweetness in his patience with the impish lad, and a true graciousness in his ability to smooth over Billie's parents' awkward gratitude.

He was a gentleman that any maiden would be proud to call husband.

For a brief, crazed moment as they had left the cottage, she had wondered why she continued to battle his offer of marriage. She enjoyed his company, she admired his intelligence, and after their kiss, she could not deny that she desperately longed for his touch.

Why not return to Kent as he requested?

Would marriage to a gentleman she considered a friend and potential lover not be preferable to the danger she courted by remaining in London? Her fantasy of glorious independence could not last forever.

Then panic had set in.

Marriage to Luce would be considerably different from sharing a few days of adventure. Once she signed the license, he would be in utter command of her life and her fortune. She would once again be under the control of a male who would possess the right to demand her absolute obedience.

What if his seeming indulgence was no more

than the desperation of a man in need of her dowry? a warning voice had whispered.

There was every possibility that once he had her in his power he would readily return to his own interests. Interests that would keep him in London and perhaps even traveling about the world. While she would once again be buried in the country with the added burden of his mother and sisters keeping a judging eye upon her every movement.

Gads, how could she take the risk?

It would shatter her heart.

No. There must be some means of winning her independence. A means that did not depend upon risking her future with Lord Calfield.

All very sensible. Unfortunately, it did not keep her from experiencing an aching pain that clutched at the center of her chest.

Lost in her thoughts, Kate barely noted her surroundings. It was not until Luce reached out to grasp her arm that she realized they had arrived at the door to his room.

Clearly sensing her distraction, he regarded her pale face with a searching gaze.

"Well, my dear, I have returned you to London, just as I promised."

"Yes," she croaked, her throat constricted as she battled the threatening tears.

Blast it all.

Luce had been right when he said that every adventure had a price. She had not known how high the cost would be.

"You have been very quiet," he accused with a gathering frown. "Are you not feeling well?"

"Of course I am." She forced herself to give a small shrug. "I have always been rather quiet."

"Perhaps before you left Kent, but you have been

very different since arriving in London." His gaze narrowed with a dangerous perception. "What is it, Kate?"

She had to get away. He knew her too well to be fooled for long. She drew in a deep breath and fought for control of her unruly emotions.

"I suppose I am rather tired. Maybe I should lie down for a bit."

His blue eyes darkened in swift concern. "If you have taken a chill, I must call the doctor. It would be foolish to take any risks."

A warmth at his ready desire to care for her rushed through her blood before she sternly took command of herself.

"No, I am merely weary from the travel."

"You are certain?"

"Yes."

"Then I will escort you."

"Luce." She paused to swallow the ridiculous lump in her throat. "I would prefer to go to my rooms alone."

He stilled, his senses on full alert. "Why? Do you fear I will press myself upon you?"

"Of course not. There is simply no need to escort me a few steps down the corridor."

"And there is nothing troubling you?"

Nothing beyond a sense of loss that felt as if it were settled in for a good long stay, she wryly acknowledged.

"Not at all," she bravely lied.

A sudden flare of anger tightened his features, assuring her that he was not fooled for a moment.

"I presumed, Kate, that I had finally convinced you that I am not the enemy. Was I mistaken?"

She bit her lip at the new edge in his tone. "Please, I do not want to discuss this now, Luce."

"Discuss what?" He reached out to cup her chin. "The fact that you are determined to judge me in your father's shadow?"

She abruptly pulled away from him. She was not prepared for their inevitable confrontation. Not now. Not when she felt vulnerable and not at all herself.

She needed time to remind herself of all the sensible reasons for not marrying this glorious gentleman.

"I just want to go to my chambers," she pleaded softly.

"Very well," he gritted out, clearly angered by her elusive manner. "We will continue this discussion over dinner."

"I cannot. I promised Lord Thorpe before I left London that I would attend the theater with him tonight."

Pure male fury hardened his expression as he took a threatening step toward her.

"So that is the reason you were so determined to leave Brighton," he rasped. "You had already made plans with your devoted rake."

"Luce," she protested, glancing down the hall to ensure they were alone. "Please do not make a scene. There are servants about."

"I do not give a damn if every servant in London is about."

"Well, I do."

"Then we will go into my chambers and discuss this in private."

She took a hasty step backward. "No."

"The devil take it, Kate. Why are you closing me out?"

"I have to go."

The muscles of his jaw knotted as he struggled to control his rising fury.

"Oh yes, I would not wish you to be late for your evening with Lord Thorpe. He does, after all, possess the good sense not to desire you as a wife. It seems a certain means of driving a gentleman mad."

Kate gave a mute shake of her head as she abruptly turned and fled down the hall.

Dear lord, what a fool she had been.

A naive, ridiculous fool.

He had been a damnable fool.

Watching Kate scurry away, Luce clenched his hands in impotent fury.

Why the hell had he pressed her?

He had known from the moment they left Brighton that something was troubling Kate. Her determined distance had been nearly palpable in the air, even when he had teasingly attempted to coax a smile to her pale face.

He should have been more patient, he chastised himself. She was wary of offering her trust to any gentleman. Her father had trained her to believe that love meant blind obedience and submission to constant judgment. It would take patience to teach her that he would never cage or condemn her.

But the moment he felt her replacing the barriers between them, he had overreacted.

Kate filled him with a joy he had never before experienced. Just having her near was enough to brighten his day. What if she decided to force him from her life? What if she decided she could never be his wife?

What if she decided Lord Thorpe might better fulfill her need for glorious adventures?

Startled by the ruthless jealousy that pierced his heart, Luce ground his teeth in frustration.

Bloody hell.

He could not lose Kate. Not now that he had discovered how deeply she had entrenched herself in his heart. Not when his soul sang when he caught a glimpse of her. Not when she made his body ache with an incessant need. Not when she filled his every thought.

She belonged to him.

Not because she could provide the money he so desperately needed. Or because she was of suitable birth and position.

She belonged to him simply because she was Kate.

With a growl, he turned on his heel and rapidly left the hotel. Perhaps he should be more patient and understanding, he grimly acknowledged as he caught the nearest hack and demanded to be taken to the docks. But he would be damned if he would stand aside and allow Kate to be seduced away by a charming rascal.

The journey did not take long. Leaving the hack, Luce crossed directly to the small pub where most of his crew preferred to gather when they were in London. Thrusting open the narrow door, he stepped into the loud, smoky public room and glanced about for Foster.

He need not have bothered. The door had barely closed behind him when he saw the craggy sailor barreling his way through the throng to stand before him with an accusing expression.

"Well, it is about bloody time. Where have you been?"

"Not now, Foster," Luce sternly halted the hovering

lecture. The elderly man had a rather annoying habit of treating him as if he were eight rather than eight and twenty. "What have you learned of Lord Thorpe?"

There was a sharp pause at his unusual lack of civility. "Has something occurred?"

Luce grimaced. "The gentleman is a blasted thorn in my side. I should like to throttle the treacherous cur."

Foster gave a lift of his shaggy brows. "Are you certain that it is Lord Thorpe who is the thorn, and not Miss Frazer?"

A rueful sigh was wrenched from his throat. Of course Kate was a thorn. A relentless, prodding thorn. She had been plaguing him from the moment he had stepped into the London garden and viewed her sitting there blithely flirting with another gentleman.

"She is proving to be somewhat trying," he admitted as he scrubbed a hand over his face. It was taking every bit of willpower not to charge back to the hotel and toss her over his shoulder. His distant ancestors clearly had the right idea in handling unruly women. "Just give me what you know of this Thorpe fellow."

There was a moment's pause before Foster at last heaved a heavy sigh. "Very well. From what I could discover, he just celebrated his thirtieth birthday and has been the target of every matchmaking mama in England since coming of age. There have been a few earlier scandals, but none that were any more than the usual antics of a wealthy nobleman, and all of them forgiven when he returned from the war as a hero."

A war hero? Gads, it made his teeth clench.

"What about his finances? Is he on the dun?"

"It is rumored that he possesses a bloody fortune."

"His family? Are they welcome among society?"

"You could say that," Foster retorted in dry tones. "His father is the Duke of Harmond and his mother is the daughter of the Earl of Coventry."

Luce abruptly dropped onto a wooden chair. So much for his fortune-hunting theory, he grimly acknowledged. The man could no doubt buy and sell him a dozen times over.

"You are certain?"

"'Taint easy to mistake the son of a Duke, Luce. I'm surprised you didn't recognize him yourself."

He should have, of course. Although he rarely attended society functions, he was a shrewd enough businessman to keep a careful account of those among the *ton* who possessed wealth or power. It was vital to cultivate such relationships whenever possible.

Now he could only presume that his wits had been too scrambled by Kate to allow his usual instincts to sense the truth. And, if he were perfectly honest, his judgment had been clouded by a healthy dose of good old-fashioned jealousy.

He wanted to believe the cad was a worthless scoundrel. It helped to make his own reasons for pursuing Kate more palatable.

"Damn," he muttered.

"Is something wrong, sir?"

He gave a sharp bark of laughter. "What could possibly be wrong, Foster? My family is in near ruin, my fiancée treats me as if I carry the pox, and she is now currently in the company of the most dashing, wealthy bachelor ever to grace England."

"Yes, well, a rather nasty bit of ill luck."

"You could say that."

Foster cleared his throat. "Mayhap it is time to consider a change of plans."

"A change of plans?"

"There is more than one wealthy maiden in London."

Luce's brows abruptly snapped together. "Good God, not again, Foster. I have told you that I do not want another. Kate is the only wife I desire."

"And if she will not have you?"

"I . . ." He swallowed the unwelcome lump that threatened to choke him. "She is merely out of her wits at the moment. Her damnable father has her utterly convinced that every man she encounters will do his best to crush her will. I must somehow prove that I can be trusted."

Foster grimaced as he lifted a hand to scratch at his thinning gray hair. "Well, you'd best do so swiftly."

Something in his gruff tone made Luce regard him with a growing concern. "What do you mean?"

With seeming reluctance, Foster reached into the pocket of his battered coat to pull out a crumpled note.

"This message came for you while you were gone. It is from your mother."

Luce's stomach clenched in chilled dread as he reached to pluck the folded paper from his friend's hand. His mother would not have written if it were not urgent. At least, not to him.

Wanting nothing more than to toss the missive into the nearby fire, he instead unfolded the paper and forced himself to read the elegant scrawl.

"Bloody hell," he muttered.

"Is it bad?"

He sucked in a deep, painful breath. "It appears that the rumors of my aborted wedding have circulated among the moneylenders and the vultures have begun to circle."

"What will you do?"

His gaze shifted to the window. It offered a view of the dark street, barely illuminated by a feeble lantern.

No doubt Kate was even now preparing for her evening with Lord Thorpe. She would be attired in some shimmering gown that would reveal far too much of her alabaster skin and bring out the flames of her titian curls.

He closed his eyes in longing.

"I must return to Kent. The sooner the better."

"Yes, sir."

Luce rose to his feet to leave the stifling atmosphere of the pub.

He had to speak with Kate. He had to somehow convince her that he could offer her a life far preferable to one of aimless adventures and independence.

Unfortunately, he had nothing to barter beyond himself. And he very much feared that it wasn't nearly enough.

He hailed a passing hack and grimly returned to the hotel.

Kate walked in a daze toward her room.

It had proved to be a most astonishing evening. Oh, it was not the rather tedious performance of *Hamlet* that had been a surprise. Nor even the elegant dinner that Lord Thorpe had ordered at one of the most expensive hotels in London.

Instead, it had been the gentleman's stern persistence when he sensed that something was troubling

her, and her own startling confessions, that had
come as such a shock.

She had not intended to admit her charade, nor
her reasons for coming to London. It was far too
dangerous to admit to anyone. But unfortunately,
she had been too vulnerable to battle his relentless questions and by the end of the evening, she
had discovered the truth tumbling from her lips
in rapid bursts.

Thank goodness he had not seemed offended by
her deceptions. He had not even attempted to
chide her for her foolishness. Instead, he had offered a measure of sincere admiration for her
daring and then, most unexpectedly of all, an irre-
sistible solution to her most pressing troubles.

Kate had reeled at his generous offer that she become a guest of his parents. As he so firmly pointed
out, her father could hardly complain at her wish
to visit the Duke and Duchess of Harmond. Not
when they possessed a spotless reputation, and
even more importantly, a most eligible son.

Sir Frazer would be delighted by the thought of
her being in such illustrious company, and she
would have ample opportunity to consider her future with no pressure of weddings or being locked
in the wine cellar.

She should have been delighted.

This was a perfect opportunity to put an end to
her farce of an engagement once and for all. Luce
would have to choose another bride soon. And her
father would certainly halt his bullying efforts if he
believed she possessed the potential to lure a future
duke up the aisle.

It was precisely what she desired, and yet she had
never been more miserable in her life.

Chastising herself for her bout of self-pity, Kate

firmly squared her shoulders and moved to her door.

She had made her decision. There would be no regrets. Soon she would forget all about Lord Calfield.

She shoved open the door and stepped inside.

"Good evening, Kate."

Her key and her reticule dropped to the carpet as she discovered Luce calmly leaning against the mantel.

"Luce," she breathed in shock. "How did you get in here?"

He gave a shrug of his shoulders as he thrust himself upright and strolled to the center of the room.

"I told the maid that you had escaped from Bedlam and I had come to take you back. She did not seem the least surprised. Indeed, she was quite anxious to be of help."

"Very amusing," she retorted, shivering at the brooding manner in which his eyes lingered upon the generous amount of skin revealed by her bronze evening gown.

He crossed his arms over his chest as his gaze slowly returned to her wary eyes.

"How was the play?"

"Adequate."

"What did you see?"

She blinked at the unexpected question, unnerved by the manner in which his coiled power filled the room.

What was he doing here?

"What?"

"The play?" he repeated in carefully controlled tones. "What did you see?"

"Oh. *Hamlet.*"

"Hardly a daring choice. I thought you wished to be adventurous?"

"It was adventurous for me. I have never seen *Hamlet* performed before."

His lips gave a reluctant twitch at her unconscious lack of sophistication.

"Ah yes, I had forgotten your limited social life."

Rubbing her hands over the bare arms that still tingled from his gaze, Kate licked her dry lips.

"What do you want?"

His stare seared over her countenance. "The truth would be a nice change."

"Truth? I . . . I have never lied to you."

"No?" He gave a short, humorless laugh. "Then tell me, Kate, why did you flee from me today? Were you truly exhausted?"

"I was tired, yes," she said, fighting a futile battle against her revealing blush.

"And there was nothing else?"

"I needed some time to consider."

"Consider what?"

The moment had come. There was no mistaking the grim determination etched onto the lean face or the pulsing tension that gripped his body.

He was not leaving until he had forced a confession, she reluctantly acknowledged. And any hope of slipping away without an angry scene was lost.

She sucked in a steadying breath.

Courage, Kate, courage, she silently reassured herself.

"I wished to consider where I would go from here."

"And have you made your decision?"

"Yes. I will leave for Devonshire tomorrow."

A taut, dangerous silence descended as he took a deliberate step forward.

"Devonshire?" he demanded with a lethal softness. "With Lord Thorpe?"

She shivered, wondering what he would say if she told him that she did not want to travel to Devonshire. Not with Lord Thorpe or anyone else.

What she wanted was to remain here with him. To pretend that he did not need her wealth and that he had tumbled madly in love with her.

He would no doubt be shocked, and also a little wary of what she expected of him. A marriage of convenience was one thing. A glorious love match was quite another.

"He has invited me to visit his parents," she instead revealed, her breath catching as he gave a deep growl and reached out to grasp her shoulders in a tight grip.

"The hell he has," he ground out, a hectic flush upon his cheekbones. "And what of us, Kate? Can you truly tell me that you feel nothing for me? That you have not enjoyed our days together? That you do not desire me?"

He was so close that she could feel the heat of his body branding her skin. She had only to lean forward to be in his arms. To feel the hard strength . . .

With a ruthless determination, she wrenched herself from his touch.

She could not weaken. Not unless she wished to find herself seduced back to Kent and the life she had left behind.

How long would it be before the regrets came crashing in? When Luce abandoned her for his business? When she found herself alone and worthless as she wandered about her empty home? When she awoke one morning to discover she was an old woman with nothing in her life but a husband who had needed her only for her wealth?

Her chin unconsciously lifted. "We have enjoyed a pleasant interlude, but I warned you from the beginning that I have no intention of marrying you, Luce. I have no intention of marrying anyone at the moment."

Luce shoved his hands through the golden hair, his nose flaring with barely controlled fury.

"Why? Why is the thought of wedding me so repugnant to you?"

"You know why, Luce."

"Because you believe I am only interested in your money? That I haven't any feelings for you?"

"In part," she agreed in a choked voice. "But more importantly, I do not wish to place myself under the authority of another. I will not be confined to Kent once again."

His eyes darkened. "And you believe that is what I will do? Take your money and then imprison you in my home?"

"You have your business that will be forever taking you to London and who knows where else. That is not even to mention the difficulties of salvaging your estate from the moneylenders. How could you possibly do anything but abandon your wife?"

If anything, her defensive words only fueled the flames of his anger.

His arms crossed over his chest as his lips twisted with a humorless smile.

"No doubt I must be mad, but I thought that you might actually desire to be at my side. Whether it was in London, or upon my ship, or even confronting the rather unpleasant moneylenders. Clearly I overrated the attractions of an impoverished earl with nothing to offer but his hand in marriage."

The edge of bitterness in his voice struck directly

in her heart. Why was he so angry? If anyone should be angry, it was she. It had been his notion to follow her to London after leaving her at the altar.

Had he stayed in Kent where he belonged, she would no doubt be enjoying a carefree, exciting stay in London. She might even have succumbed to Lord Thorpe's charming flirtation.

Certainly, she would not be wretched and confused and not at all confident that she was making the proper decision.

"What do you want from me?" she at last demanded in shaky tones.

"I want you to give up this foolishness," he ground out. "I want you to return to Kent and be my wife."

Her hand lifted to press against her throat that ached with unshed tears.

"It is not foolishness, and if you truly cared for me you would understand my desires."

He stared at her as if he thought she had lost her mind.

And perhaps she had, she acknowledged with a hysterical urge to laugh.

What maiden in her proper senses tossed aside a handsome earl who made her feel as if she were the most cherished, the most witty, the most beautiful person on the face of the earth? A man who had proved he could be kind and tender and charmingly impulsive.

A woman who did not want her heart ripped out and stomped upon, she sternly reminded herself.

"So you refuse to wed me?" he demanded.

"Yes."

"With no regrets?"

She forced herself to turn away from that searing

gaze, knowing she could not hide the agony gnawing at her heart.

"I am sorry, Luce, but I am certain that you will soon enough discover another wealthy maiden to take my place."

There was a stunned silence at her accusation. Then, with a rasping breath, Luce moved to wrench open the door.

"The devil I will," he snapped. "I hope you find what you are searching for, Kate."

She flinched as the door was slammed shut, and she was left alone with her pain.

"So do I," she whispered, unable to shake the sensation that she had just made the greatest mistake of her life.

CHAPTER ELEVEN

As ill luck would have it, Kate did not leave London the next morning. Before she had even managed to enjoy her breakfast, she received a brief note from Lord Thorpe revealing that unexpected business had forced him to remain in town for several more days and apologizing for the delay.

Disappointed but resigned, Kate had been forced to consider her options. Her first instinct, of course, had been to remain safely hidden within her chambers until Lord Thorpe could take her away from London. The mere thought of accidentally crossing paths with Luce was enough to make her feel ill.

She had hurt him. Oh, no doubt it was only his pride, but it was enough to make him regard her with a fiery dislike that she could not bear.

Thankfully, common sense had come to her rescue. She had only a few days left in London. And goodness only knew if she would ever be allowed to return.

She would not be confined to her chambers. Not by Lord Calfield or anyone else.

Her determination, or perhaps stubborn stupidity, lingered for the next several days, prompting her to an endless round of sightseeing, lectures, and intellectual salons. The hectic pace, however, did not prevent her from incessantly glancing over her shoulder as if she feared the golden-haired pirate might suddenly appear. Nor did it keep her long nights from being haunted by dreams of his tender kindness.

She had presumed that the passing days would ease the strange ache that clenched at her heart. Or at least dim the remembrance of their days together.

Instead, it seemed that his lingering presence was everywhere. It was in the garden when she desired a breath of fresh air. It was at the theater where he had followed her to disrupt her evening with Lord Thorpe. And most of all, it was in her chambers, where he had so tenderly cared for her after her night of overindulgence.

It was little wonder she was so anxious to leave London and travel to Devonshire where she could at last put Lord Calfield firmly from her mind.

Well, perhaps he would not be gone from her mind, she ruefully conceded, but at least she would halt glancing over her shoulder and peeking about corners as if she were batty.

Returning to the hotel after yet another exhausting day, Kate discovered herself breathing a sigh of relief when a maid scurried to her side to reveal that a gentleman was awaiting her in the back parlor.

Lord Thorpe, at last.

Not even bothering to visit her chambers to remove her cape and bonnet, Kate hurried toward the back of the hotel, which sported a small but nicely private parlor. She could only hope that Lord Thorpe had not come to reveal he would be unable to escort her to Devonshire. Whatever her lack of enthusiasm for staying at a palatial ducal mansion with utter strangers, the option was certainly preferable to remaining in London with the constant danger of encountering Luce.

Pressing open the door, Kate stepped into the room with a forced smile of greeting.

"At last, my lord, I feared you had . . ." Her light words came to a startled halt as she regarded the short, solidly-built gentleman with a shock of gray hair and a countenance that appeared to have been carved from granite. This was most certainly not the elegant Lord Thorpe. Indeed, he appeared more a ruffian than a gentleman. "Oh. Forgive me. There must have been some mistake."

About to back from the room, Kate was halted when the man took an abrupt step forward, holding up a gnarled hand.

"Please, Miss Frazer, I would ask for just a moment of your time."

The sound of her name stopped her retreat and Kate regarded the craggy features more closely. There was something vaguely familiar about him . . .

It took a long moment before she abruptly recalled where she had seen the man before.

"You work for Lord Calfield," she muttered.

"Aye. My name is Foster."

With jerky movements, Kate untied her bonnet and removed it from her curls. She needed an opportunity to gain command of her thundering heart.

"I suppose he sent you here?" she at last demanded.

"Bloody he . . . I mean, good God, no." The sailor gave an embarrassed cough before continuing. "He would gut me like a fish if he even suspected I was here."

The sharp twinge she felt in the region of her heart was not disappointment, she sternly reassured herself. The last thing she desired was interference from Luce.

Still, she discovered herself sinking into the nearest chair, almost as if her knees had suddenly gone weak.

"If you are not here for Lord Calfield, then what brings you to the hotel?"

The man absently rumpled his gray hair, as if he were uncertain himself why he had come.

"Mayhap I should first warn you that Luce is more than just an employer to me," he muttered in abrupt tones that revealed he was not at all comfortable in the presence of a woman. Or perhaps it was simply *her* presence. "Five years ago he found me in the stews drinking my way through most of the gin in London. He had heard I once sailed at the side of Nelson, and despite all rumors that I had gone to rubble after leaving the navy, he believed I possessed the skills to be his captain." There was a short silence before the man roughly cleared his throat. "He saved my life on that day. I should no doubt be lying in the gutter, if not in my grave, if he had not given me a reason to pull myself out of the pub."

Despite herself, Kate discovered her heart warming at Luce's kindness. She could just imagine him bullying the poor drunken sailor into taking command of his ship. Whatever his faults, he did not consider himself above others, and was obviously loyal to those who had earned his trust.

Trust.

She suppressed a heavy sigh. Trust seemed to be the one thing she lacked in abundance.

"Obviously you are quite attached to Lu . . . Lord Calfield," she murmured.

"I would gladly take a bullet for him," Foster

retorted with a grimace. "Hell's teeth, I'd as soon take a bullet as be here."

She blinked at the odd words. "I fear I do not understand."

He folded his arms across his barrel chest, his eyes narrowing as he regarded her puzzled expression.

"I warned him about you, Miss Frazer. I knew the moment he began chasing after you and behaving the fool that he was headed for trouble. But like any man bewitched by a female, he refused to listen to reason."

"Bewitched?" Kate pressed a hand to her suddenly unstable heart. "You are mistaken, Mr. Foster. Lord Calfield was never bewitched, merely in desperate need of funds."

The older man's expression hardened with obvious anger. "If that were true, he would not have trailed behind you like a well-heeled hound, Miss. Nor would he have neglected his business and family simply to please you." His lips thinned until they nearly disappeared. "You are not the only rich maiden in England, Miss Frazer. Had his wits not been so clouded with the need to make you his wife, he would already be happily wed to another."

Abruptly rising to her feet, Kate regarded the intruder with flashing eyes. How dare he? Why, he implied that she had deliberately toyed with Luce's emotions merely for her own pleasure. And that it was somehow her fault he was too stubborn to choose a maiden more willing.

"I assure you that I never attempted to deceive Lord Calfield," she gritted. "I made it quite clear from the moment he arrived in London that I no longer desired to be his wife. Indeed, I did everything possible to convince him to seek another."

Foster offered a disgusted snort at her clipped words. "All the while you flirted and teased and readily allowed yourself to be in his company. Do not forget, I witnessed the two of you together. It did not seem you were anxious to be rid of him."

Ridiculously, a warm blush filled her cheeks. "Certainly he is a charming companion, and annoyingly persistent. What would you have me do? Give him the cut direct?"

"Yes. A swift stroke would have been kinder in the end."

Blast it all. Why should she feel guilty? She had not left him humiliated at the altar. She had not followed and plagued him about London. She had not pretended to care for him when all she desired was his wealth.

"Whatever you may believe, I have not attempted to halt Lord Calfield from finding the dowry he so desperately needs. Indeed, I have not even spoken with him for the past week," she said stiffly. "I do not doubt he is already sweeping his way through the ballrooms of London and breaking dozens of hearts."

Foster took a step forward, his expression tight with suspicion. For a moment, Kate feared that he might have sensed the jealousy that ripped through her heart at the mere thought of Luce charming another. Then he gave a slow shake of his head.

"You do not know?"

"Know? Know what?"

"Luce has left London. He returned to Kent days ago."

Kate caught her breath in shock. Gads, the revelation should have brought a sense of glorious relief. She could leave her chambers without the constant dread of meeting him in the corridor.

She could sleep easily at night and enjoy her days of independence.

Ah yes, she should be delighted.

Instead, a deep, icy sense of loss abruptly settled into her very bones.

"But . . ." She gave a slow shake of her head, wondering how she had not known. How she had not sensed his absence. "Surely he should have remained in London if he desires a bride?"

His scowl only became more pronounced. "He has put off all thoughts of marriage. Hardly surprising after having his heart stomped upon."

Kate ignored his ridiculous accusation that she could ever reach Luce's distant heart.

"I thought it was imperative that he wed. What of his father's debts?"

"They remain, although he has managed to put off the most pressing of his creditors by offering his shipping company for sale. He hopes the profits will gain him time to find another means of rescuing his family."

He was selling his shipping company?

Kate abruptly fell back into her seat. Dear Lord. Why? Those ships were everything to him. Not only financially, but as tangible proof that he could forge his own path despite his father's condemnation.

"This is absurd," she muttered. "There are any number of maidens who would be delighted to trade their dowry for the title Countess."

Foster gave a growl that might have indicated disgust. "So I told him, any number of times. I even made him a list of eligible possibilities. But would he listen to me? Fah. He had it in his head that you were to be his bride and no other would do. Now, see what has happened."

Kate gave a slow shake of her head. It was all so

vastly confusing. Not only Luce's abrupt return to Kent, but his selling the business he treasured.

Why had he not sought out a more willing maiden? Or even continued his pursuit of her?

It was not at all the behavior of a gentleman who was only interested in a convenient means of acquiring a fortune.

She pressed her fingers to her throbbing temples as the older man glared at her with a steady anger.

"What do you want from me?"

Foster jutted his chin to a stubborn angle. "I want you to talk with him. To convince him once and for all that you are never going to be his wife. Mayhap then he will come to his senses and seek another before he has lost everything."

"I . . ."

Her words faltered quite simply because she did not know what to say. Her thoughts were too tangled. And her heart . . .

Damn it all. Her heart felt as if it were being ripped from her chest as she thought of Luce proudly turning his back on London and sacrificing everything he possessed because he could not bear to think of another woman as his countess.

"Well?" the sailor prompted in gruff tones.

Not even realizing she had made a decision, Kate slowly lifted her head, a single tear tracing its way down her cheek.

"I will go to Kent."

Foster heaved a deep sigh. "Thank God."

"Thank God." Pressing a fluttering hand to her heart, the current Countess of Calfield pounced upon Luce the moment he entered the door. "I have been awaiting you for hours. Why are you never here when I need you?"

Biting back a caustic comment, Luce forced himself to ease his raw nerves. He had known when he returned to Kent without the fortune he needed that it would be difficult. Especially for his mother, who had always refused to face the truth of their financial ruin. It was far easier to pretend that all was well than to actually have to make the sacrifices that were so obviously necessary.

"Someone had to speak with the grocer. He insisted upon payment before he would continue our credit," he said with admirable calm. "What do you need?"

Lady Calfield waved a dismissive hand, as if having food upon the table were of little importance. "Thomas came to me this morning and said that a gentleman had arrived to view the stables."

Luce smiled with grim amusement. He should have known that his mother's loyal servants would be tattling behind his back. They would have to suspect that his efforts of economy would soon affect their own positions.

"Yes, it is a Mr. Marrow. He is interested in making an offer on father's hunters as well as the carriages."

"Luce." Horrified shock touched the aging countenance, marring the fading beauty. "You cannot mean to sell the carriages?"

He crossed his arms over his chest, steeling his courage. Too long he had dodged the painful choices that had to be made. He could not waver now.

"They will go along with the grooms and trainers. We will keep two horses and the small cart."

"Cart? You expect your sisters to travel about in a cart? They will be humiliated."

Luce lifted a shoulder. "They can walk if they prefer."

"Dear heavens. How can you be so heartless? Your father . . ."

"My father is the reason we are currently in this mess, Mother," he interrupted in firm tones. He was in no humor to hear of the glorious generosity of his father, who had fribbled away near sixty thousand pounds. "And I fear this is only the beginning. I intend to review the servants this evening and request that those who are not essential to the running of the household search for another position."

A petulant anger flashed in Lady Calfield's blue eyes. "None of this would have been necessary if you had done your duty and wed Miss Frazer as you were supposed to. Now we all must suffer for your selfishness."

Luce flinched as if he had been slapped. It was not guilt. At least not guilt for having allowed Kate to slip from his fingers. Over the past few days, he had come to realize that wedding Kate would have been a ghastly mistake. No matter what his feelings for her, the knowledge that he had been in need of her wealth would have always lain between them.

How could she ever truly place her trust in him? Or ever give him her heart?

She deserved better. She deserved the happiness that had been missing from her life for too long.

His noble determination, however, did not make him miss her any less, or ease the sense of loneliness that plagued him with ruthless intensity.

"Perhaps it is selfish, mother, but I refuse to become a damnable leech upon Sir Frazer simply because you desire your carriages and French maid." He squared his shoulders, a fierce pride etched upon his countenance. "For once, an Earl of Calfield will pay his own debts, not sell his soul to take the easy path."

Not surprisingly, his mother was far from impressed by his lofty morals. She was a creature of comfort and luxury. The mere thought of maintaining a bit of economy was enough to make her break out in a rash.

"And what of me and your sisters? Will you see us dressed in rags and tending the fields like common peasants?"

His lips reluctantly twitched at the shrill accusation. "Not unless you possess a particular desire to plow fields. Of course, if you have a hankering to be of assistance, there are several cottages in need of new thatching."

Lady Calfield stomped her foot in fury. "This is not amusing, Luce. And I warn you, I will not tolerate living like a beggar. If need be, I will take the girls to my sister's in Surrey. I will not have them a source of pity throughout the neighborhood."

"As you will." Luce thrust a weary hand through his golden hair. He had devoted twenty hours a day to just keeping the wolves at bay. He did not possess the strength to battle his mother as well. "I will not pretend that things are not bad, mother. Nor that they will soon improve. All I can promise is that I will do everything in my power to ensure the future is better."

"Everything but wed a maiden who could easily restore our fortunes to what they should be," she said with a disdainful sniff.

"Everything but that."

She glared at him for a long moment before

turning to flounce up the stairs. "Then stay here and watch your father's estate crumble to dust," she charged over her shoulder. "And know that your pride has no doubt ruined any hope for your sisters' future."

With a deep sigh, Luce turned to leave the house. There was still Mr. Morrow to deal with in the stables, and several tenants awaiting the opportunity to air their grievances. It would be another long day, not improved by the realization that he would have to confront servants who had devoted their entire lives to the Calfield family and request that they pack their bags and leave.

It was enough to make a gentleman consider boarding the nearest ship and never looking back, he acknowledged. Then an unwittingly grim smile touched his lips. Unfortunately for him, he no longer possessed any ships.

Refusing to dwell upon his dark thoughts, Luce crossed the yard toward the nearby stables. It was enough to concentrate upon the troubles at hand without borrowing regrets from the past.

At least if Mr. Morrow was willing to purchase the contents of the stable, they would have enough blunt to stave off the most pressing creditors. Hopefully, by then he would have an offer for his business that would keep them afloat until harvest. A small miracle in itself.

Rounding the crumbling fountain in the center of the yard, Luce was just passing the main gate when the sound of approaching footsteps stopped him. Since the estate was set off from the main path by a long, oak-lined drive, he knew whoever was approaching must be a visitor to Calfield Park. Or, more likely, another creditor, he ruefully acknowledged.

His first impulse was to hurry on to the stables and ignore whatever new disaster might loom on the horizon. His current temper was not best suited to pandering to the shrill demands and threats of yet another merchant. Then he gave a resigned shake of his head.

He was not his father. He would not dodge and evade his responsibilities and pretend that tomorrow would take care of itself.

At least not any longer.

Squaring his shoulders, he moved firmly toward the gate, reaching it at nearly the precise moment as the approaching guest. His eyes abruptly widened. Bloody hell, this was not the burly merchant he had expected. Instead the visitor was slender and young and utterly female.

The determined smile that he had pasted to his lips faltered at the same moment as his heart.

Kate . . .

Unwittingly, he reached out his hand to grasp the rough stone of the gate. His knees did not feel at all steady and his thoughts were clouded with disbelieving surprise. In truth, he felt as if he had just been hit on the head with a spade.

A large spade.

Slowly, his gaze traveled over her stiff form, noting the return of her prim blue gown and sensible wool cape. Even the beautiful titian curls had been ruthlessly hidden beneath a bonnet that was more suited to an aging matron than a lovely young maiden.

The daring, exotic creature of London had been returned to the sensible, shy spinster he recalled from their first meeting.

A pang that might have been regret clutched at his heart before he sternly grasped control of his scattered senses. Damn it all, this woman had dangled him, tortured him, and crushed his heart.

He was not about to allow her to continue with her painful games.

"Miss Frazer," he said in cold tones. "What a very unexpected surprise."

Her breath seemed to catch at the chill in the air, which had little to do with the stiff northerly breeze.

"Good day, my lord. I hope I do not intrude?"

His jaw tightened at her determined politeness. Did she expect him to treat her as if they were no more than distant acquaintances? Well, he was not near gentlemanly enough for that.

"What are you doing here?"

She paused, as if caught off guard by his clipped question. "I was passing by and I thought . . ."

"No," he intruded, his throat oddly raw as his gaze hungrily roamed over the pale features and eyes that appeared a misty blue. Gads, he had not realized just how much it would hurt to see her again. "It is impossible to simply pass by Calfield Park. You must have a reason for coming here."

A sharp silence descended before Kate gave a nervous cough. "I . . . I seem to have caught you at a bad moment. Forgive me."

Luce knew he was behaving the boor. But it seemed impossible to conjure a measure of graciousness. Not when her mere presence was twisting his insides into mush.

"I thought you were traveling to Devonshire." He abruptly broke the silence.

"I decided it was best to return to Kent."

"I must admit that I am rather surprised." He could not entirely keep an edge of bitterness from his voice. "I thought you were quite anxious to be

swept off your feet by your devoted duke-in-waiting.
Did he abandon you, or did you decide a stuffy
ducal palace did not fit in with your notion of a friv-
olous adventure?"

Kate stiffened at his sudden thrust. "Neither."

"Then why would you be here? You made it clear
you would rather be hauled to the gallows than to
return."

Her tongue reached out to wet her lips in a nervous fashion. Luce shivered as his gaze lingered
upon the tempting shimmer. He remembered the
precise taste of that sweet mouth.

"I had a visit from Mr. Foster."

Luce froze in icy shock. "Foster?"

"Yes . . . he was concerned and requested that I
return to Kent to speak with you."

He flinched in dismay. Blast his interfering, busy-
body captain. How dare he interfere? This entire
situation was difficult enough without knowing
Kate was close at hand to see his pathetic struggles.

"Foster is worse than any mother hen, I fear," he
retorted in stiff tones. "If he disturbed you, I apologize."

"He did not disturb me." She searched his
guarded expression, as if attempting to determine
his inner thoughts. "At least his visit did not disturb
me. It was his revelations that I discovered troubling. Is it true you are selling your shipping
company?"

Luce gritted his teeth until tight knots formed in
his jaws. At this moment, he would have happily
ordered Foster to walk the plank.

The last thing in the world he desired was this
woman's damnable pity. "That is surely no one's
concern but my own, Miss Frazer."

She bit her lip at his obvious dismissal. "Perhaps.

That does not halt me, however, from being concerned. I know how much those ships mean to you."

A flare of fury raced through him. Of course the company had meant a great deal to him. It had given him a purpose in life that had been sorely missing. But the loss of his company was nothing in comparison with the aching loss of this woman.

A loss that she had not even acknowledged, dash it all.

"Actually, you seem to know very little, Miss Frazer. Not about me or my company."

"Luce . . ."

Drawing in a deep breath, he forced a bored expression to his countenance. He would not endure her sympathy. Anything but that.

"I fear that you have come at a rather inconvenient time, Miss Frazer," he said in brisk tones. "I think it best if you return home and allow me to continue with my duties."

"I see." Her eyes seemed to darken, almost as if he had managed to wound her with his dismissal. "I offer my apologies. I did not intend to disrupt your day."

She had disrupted more than his day, Luce grimly acknowledged. She had disrupted the smallest progress he had made to dismissing her from his thoughts and convincing himself that his life was much better without her.

"On the next occasion perhaps it would be best if you would send word before arriving," he forced himself to say in cool tones. "The household is not currently capable of entertaining unexpected guests."

The blood drained from her countenance, leaving her nearly ashen. His heart squeezed with a ravaging pain.

"Of course." Swallowing heavily, she gave a jerky nod of her head. "Do not fear, my lord, I will not intrude again."

She turned upon her heel to leave and before he could even think to halt his impulsive movement, Luce had shifted to block her path. Suddenly, he had to know what had happened to her glorious adventures and, perhaps more importantly, Lord Thorpe.

"Is the devoted Lord Thorpe still trailing behind you, or have you sent him upon his way as well?" he demanded without warning.

For a moment, he thought she might refuse to answer, then her chin tilted so that she could stab him with an angry glare.

"Lord Thorpe is still in London," she said with as much dignity as possible.

"Poor idiot. I really should have warned him of your tendency to dangle susceptible gentlemen upon your hook before tossing them back to sea."

She flinched at the ugly accusation. "That is utterly unfair, my lord."

His lips twisted. "Is it?"

"Yes." She looked as if she were battling the urge to slap him. "I was honest from the beginning of our relationship. I never wished to hurt or deceive you. I was not the one who insisted that you remain in London, nor that you continue to pursue me. Indeed, I suggested on more than one occasion that you seek out another to wed."

Luce caught his breath at the accusation, knowing that there was no reasonable means of denying her words. She had not deliberately toyed with his emotions. Nor had she ever suggested that she would wish him as a husband.

Still, she had managed to rip out his heart. Surely that deserved some sort of punishment?

"At the same time you were quite willing to take advantage of my presence when you found it convenient, were you not, my sweet?"

"I did not come here to argue with you, Luce." She deliberately glanced toward the lane he was blocking. "Will you excuse me?"

He offered a mocking bow as he stepped to the side. "Please do not let me keep you." He waited until she was right beside him before he leaned to whisper directly in her ear. "Did you find it, Kate?"

She faltered at his soft question. "Find what?"

"Whatever it was that you were searching for."

She could not disguise the utter despair that darkened her eyes to pools of haunted green. "No. No, I did not."

Clutching her skirts, she fled down the path, unaware of the shock that held him motionless as he watched her retreat.

Dear God. She had looked almost . . . heartbroken.

CHAPTER TWELVE

Not slowing her frantic pace until she was well out of sight of Lord Calfield, Kate at last came to a halt to lean against a large oak tree. She closed her eyes and allowed the threatening tears to fall freely down her cheeks.

Oh, blast it all. Why had she come?

Because she had felt a measure of sympathy for Luce? Because she could not entirely dismiss a sense of guilt at his current plight? Because she was concerned for a friend?

Those were the reasons she had given herself on the long trek to Calfield Park. All perfectly logical reasons.

And perfectly logical lies.

She had come for one reason and one reason only.

Because for all her proud claims that she would not be wed for her wealth, for all her insistence that she was determined to live a life of adventure, what she hungered for was love.

A simple, uncomplicated love that did not demand obedience or make her constantly fear that she was about to disappoint. A love that filled her heart and her life with the contentment she had been seeking.

She wanted Luce to love her as she loved him.

Fool. Fool. Fool.

Forcing herself to straighten before she froze to the tree in the chilled breeze, Kate reluctantly continued back toward her father's estate. Luce had made it painfully obvious that he did not welcome her reappearance back into his life.

And in truth, she could not blame him.

She had been brutally clear that she would never trust him. And that she intended to leave London with Lord Thorpe. No gentleman, especially not one with Luce's pride, would readily forgive such insults.

Why had she been so stubborn? She had driven away the one gentleman who had ever shown such patience, such kindness, and such tender concern. And all because of callow fear.

Shivering, she bent her head and plodded onward. At least she should be relieved that her father appeared unaware of her brief days of rebellion, she sternly told herself. Her return had inspired no more than a rather mild lecture upon traveling home without the proper attendants, and a warning that she must be vigilant in avoiding undue attention. She had, after all, possessed the bad taste to allow herself to be abandoned at the altar. It would not do to stir up the unpleasant gossip by any forward behavior.

For once, she had allowed his words to simply flow over her. Somehow her brief taste of independence had given her the insight to believe that her father did not deliberately attempt to hurt her. In his own way, he did care for her. It was simply because he had been so deeply betrayed by her mother that he feared to trust again.

Just as she had feared.

Heaving a faint sigh, she at last came in view of

the small but meticulously tidy manor house. Despite its age, Rosehill maintained an air of pristine care and obvious wealth. A decided contrast to the vast but rambling estate she had just left behind. An estate clearly upon the edge of ruin.

Kate ruthlessly squelched the pain that threatened to bloom in the region of her heart. Calfield Park, or anything else related to Luce, was not her concern, as he had so succinctly reminded her. Not anymore.

Crossing the path that led toward the back of the estate, she used a side door to enter the house. She had expected to discover the small parlor empty at such an hour, and her heart sank as Julia abruptly rose from a chair near the window to regard her with concern.

She had hoped to escape to her bedchamber. At least until she had managed to have a good cry and somehow regained command of her wounded composure.

Now she was forced to paste a stiff smile to her lips. "Good morning, Julia."

"Kate." Moving forward, Julia narrowed her gaze, clearly not at all fooled by her casual manner. "I have been searching for you since breakfast. Where have you been?"

"I decided upon a stroll."

The dark-haired woman glanced in surprise at the frost-kissed windows. "It is rather chilled for such an early stroll, is it not?"

Kate shrugged, hiding her expression as she turned to remove the bonnet from her curls. "You know the cold has never troubled me. And I felt the need for some fresh air."

"Obviously, you felt the need for a great deal of fresh air. You have been gone near two hours."

Rather annoyed by being put through the Inquisition when she only wished to flee to the privacy of her room, Kate abruptly frowned at her cousin.

"I am not a child, Julia. If I desire to stroll for two hours, there is no reason I should not be allowed to do so," she said in exasperated tones.

Julia abruptly wrinkled her nose as she realized that she had been more than a tad intrusive. "Forgive me, Kate. You are correct. But I was concerned."

"Concerned? Why ever would you be concerned?"

There was a moment of silence, as if her cousin were carefully considering her response. "I have watched you since your return and I am worried. You barely touched your dinner last evening or your breakfast this morning, you clearly did not sleep more than a few minutes, and you have muttered less than a half a dozen words. Now you suddenly disappear for hours on end. Can you blame me for being concerned?"

Feeling somewhat abashed at having worried her dear cousin, Kate offered a faintly embarrassed smile. "Forgive me, Julia. I fear I have not yet adjusted to being home."

Julia stepped closer, reaching out to grasp her cold hands. "And you are certain that is all it is?"

She swallowed heavily. "Of course. What else could it be?"

"Well, if I were to hazard a guess, I would say it was Lord Calfield."

Kate froze at the soft words. "What?"

"Kate, I went to the hotel to visit you while I was still in London and discovered that you had left town with a Lord Calfield and were not expected back for several days." Julia captured her unwilling gaze. "Now when the earl suddenly returns to

Kent, you return as well. I do not believe it is mere coincidence."

"I . . ." Kate licked her dry lips. "I could not remain in London forever."

Julia gave a lift of her brows. "And your distraction has nothing whatsoever to do with your former fiancé?"

"Julia, really." Pulling her hands free, Kate turned to move across the room. "There is nothing at all between Lord Calfield and me."

"Even though he followed you to London? Even though you disappeared with him for several days? Even though I suspect you went to call on him this morning?"

Her eyes slid closed as she fought back the wall of pain that hit her at the memory of her brief encounter with Luce. Dear Lord, he had been so cold. So utterly dismissive. Almost as if he hated her.

"Please, Julia, I cannot discuss this now," she whispered in broken tones.

"Kate." Slowly crossing the room, her cousin placed warm hands upon her shoulders. "Then there is something?"

"No . . . I mean, he did try to convince me to wed him, but I refused." She shuddered as her heart clenched in regret. "I was so afraid that he only wanted me for my fortune."

"And now you believe you might have been mistaken?"

A sad smile curled her lips. "Yes, but in truth it no longer matters. Whatever his reason for wanting me as his bride, I realize now that no one could have offered me greater happiness. When I am with him, I feel beautiful and clever and desirable. More than that, I feel comfortable in a manner I have never before experienced. As if he accepts me precisely as I am."

"Oh, my dear. It cannot be too late," Julia said softly. "If you would speak with him . . ."

"No." Kate abruptly turned to meet the startled dark eyes. "It is not to be, Julia."

"How can you be so certain?"

"He has made it very clear that he no longer has an interest in having me as his wife." The tears once again threatened and Kate pressed a hand to her quivering stomach. "Now, please, I only wish to retire to my room until luncheon."

Julia bit her lip but gave a slow nod of her head. "Of course. If you need me, I will be here."

"Thank you."

With an unsteady smile of gratitude, Kate made her way through the room and toward the wide staircase. She knew that Julia was concerned, but at the moment she had no means of reassuring her. Not while her heart was breaking and her nerves were still raw with Luce's rejection.

Blast it all. Why had she ever returned to Kent?

Why the devil had she ever returned to Kent?

Luce's mood, which had already been dark, became positively nasty as he attempted to put Kate from his mind and complete the endless list of duties awaiting his attention.

Dammit all. Was it not bad enough he had spent the week wracked by a sense of aching loss? Or that it had taken every ounce of willpower not to follow Kate to Devonshire and plead for her to allow him a place in her life, no matter how small?

Surely he did not deserve the torture of knowing she was so close and yet unattainable?

Was she deliberately attempting to taunt him? To toy with the raw emotions that refused to heal?

As the long day passed, however, his self-righteous anger began to lessen and his thoughts turned to the reasons for Kate's unexpected return.

Why was she in Kent? Had she not made it clear she intended to travel to Devonshire with the eager Lord Thorpe at her side?

And more importantly, why had she come to Calfield Park?

Was it merely pity that had led her to brave the chilled air? Or was it something more? Could that darkness in her eyes when she denied having found what she was searching for have been regret?

He grimly attempted to still the flutters of hope deep within him. He had already allowed Kate to rip out his heart and stomp upon it once. Did he truly desire to offer it up for her punishment again?

Only a fool did not learn from his mistakes.

As darkness descended and the soft bustle of the household faded to silence, Luce found himself alone in his library. There were any number of tasks demanding his attention. Indeed, his desk was near overflowing with ledger books, lists of necessary repairs to the various cottages, the bills that had arrived that day, and a stack of journals that revealed the latest farming techniques.

And of course, he did not doubt his mother and sisters were poised just outside the door, prepared to continue their shrill insistence that they could not possibly be expected to live as paupers, despite the fact that that was precisely what they were.

For the moment, all of his troubles were meaningless. He could concentrate on nothing but Kate and her unexpected arrival at Calfield Park.

Bloody hell, he had to know.

Perhaps he was a fool. Perhaps he was only opening himself up for more disappointment. But how could he possibly go through his life if he was plagued with the constant worry he had tossed aside all hope for happiness?

He had already wasted an entire day on the blasted woman. How many more days stretched before him?

Furious with himself and even more so with the woman who had turned his life into this devilish quagmire, Luce abruptly crossed the library and jerked open the door. As expected, his mother nearly tumbled across the threshold, and he smiled grimly as she hastily attempted to appear as if she had not had her ear pressed to the heavy oak panels.

"Luce, there you are." Nervously smoothing her hands over her skirts, she regarded him with a small sniff. "I began to think you intended to lock yourself in there for the entire evening."

It certainly had crossed his mind, Luce ruefully acknowledged. He would gladly spend the night in the stables if it would ensure that he was not subjected to another tearful scene.

"Not now, mother," he sternly cut off the angry words trembling upon her lips. "I have something that needs my attention."

Her brows snapped together at his imperious tone. "At this time of night? Ridiculous. There is nothing that cannot wait until morning."

The image of a pale, beautiful countenance with wounded eyes rose to mind. Gads, he would go mad if he could not see Kate.

"No. It cannot wait."

"But I must speak with you. Nothing can be more important than the needs of your sisters."

"Actually there is nothing more important than

this. Not Calfield Park, not you, and not my sisters." A grim expression hardened his features. "It has taken too long to realize the truth."

"Really, Luce." His mother appeared shocked by his blunt confession. "How can you be so cruel? I cannot think what your father would say."

"Since father never once bothered with this estate or his family, I cannot conceive that he would say much of anything." Luce squared his shoulders, not about to be delayed another moment. "Do not fear, mother, I don't intend to abandon you to the wolves. But neither will I allow the only wonderful thing in my life to slip away without a fight. I must go."

Leaving his mother floundering in shock, Luce easily swept past her and headed for the foyer. He paused only long enough to gather his greatcoat and gloves before hurrying out of the house and toward the stables. There was an exasperating delay as he attempted to saddle his mount while the sleepy groom protested at not being allowed to perform his duty, but within a few moments he was at last on his way toward Kate's home.

As he rode through the frosty night air, it occurred to him that it was far too late for a proper call, but that did not slow his steady progress. He had to speak with Kate. He could not waste one further moment.

Nearly consumed by his pulsing yearning, Luce left the main road and crossed over the meadows and fields that surrounded Rosehill. Then, leaving his mount tethered just outside the formal gardens, he stealthily made his way to the main house. Once there, he did not even hesitate to slip through a servant's passage and up the back steps to the upper chambers.

What was a bit of trespassing between ex-fiancés?

Wincing at every creaking floorboard and silently cursing his heavy boots, which were not at all suited to sneaking about darkened corridors, he made his way toward the east wing of the house. He vaguely recalled Kate once mentioning that her chamber overlooked the rose garden, which would place it at the end of the long corridor. Halting at the last door, he paused. He could only hope that she had not changed rooms and, of course, that she was currently alone.

To simply enter the chamber was a risk, certainly. If he happened in upon Sir Frazer, it would be a bloody scandal.

And he was not wedding Lord Frazer, no matter what his fortune, he assured himself in a lame attempt to lighten the ball of terror lodged in the pit of his stomach.

Feeling more uncertain and fearful than he had ever before in his life, Luce forced his stiff hand to rise and turn the knob. Then, with a deep breath, he pushed open the door and stepped over the threshold. A swift glance revealed the large bed was empty, as was the chaise beside the window. It was the faint glow of a candle that at last drew his attention to the distant corner where Kate was seated before a mirror as she slowly brushed out the titian curls.

In the flickering light, she might have been a siren rising from the shadows. Her skin was a pure alabaster revealed in glorious perfection by the brevity of her linen shift, her eyes were a mysterious green in the reflection, and her satin curls a halo of flame.

Luce felt his world halt.

He could not move. Could not speak. He forgot even to breath.

Then, as if sensing his presence, Kate slowly turned to regard him with wide, disbelieving eyes.

"Luce?" she whispered.

Clearing his deranged thoughts enough to close the door, Luce uneasily moved to the center of the room. Beyond the predictable shock at his improper intrusion into her chamber, it was impossible to determine if she was pleased or horrified by his presence.

At last coming to a halt, he forced himself to glance about the elegant room. Anything to keep from staring at her like a lovesick fool.

Surprisingly, there was little of Kate to be seen. Oh, the furnishings were all suitably expensive and situated in the proper positions, but the personal frills and baubles that inevitably littered his sisters' rooms were oddly missing.

"Do you know this is not at all what I expected from your bedchamber? It is very . . ."

"Dull?" She supplied in oddly bitter tones. "Predictable? Boring?"

He slowly turned to face her, his body instinctively tightening as an avalanche of unwelcome sensations assaulted him.

He sternly reined in his unruly emotions.

"Impersonal. Do you not have any paintings or mementos that women always use to clutter their surroundings?"

She shrugged. "I have never felt the need to trouble with such things."

Of course, he thought with a sharp pang. A woman only fussed and altered a place she considered her own. To Kate, this estate had been her father's domain. For her, it was more a place of confinement than a home.

"I suppose you have not," he said softly, his gaze drifting over her wary countenance. "This chamber has never truly belonged to you, has it, Kate?"

She blinked, as if startled by his insight, and then, with jerky movements, she moved toward a chair to grasp her night rail and pulled it over her thin shift.

"You should not be here, Luce. If anyone were to discover you . . ."

"I do not care if all of England were to discover me here." He stepped forward, his expression somber. "I have to know why you returned to Kent."

Her breath caught at the abrupt question. "What?"

"Why did you return home?"

"I . . ." She wrapped her arms about her waist, her expression uncertain. "I realized that I could not hide forever."

Luce arched a disbelieving brow. "Perhaps not forever, but Lord Thorpe was quite eager to afford you several more weeks of unabated freedom at his ducal estate. Why did you toss that aside?"

She licked her lips in an uneasy manner. Good, he thought with grim satisfaction. He damn well hoped she was perturbed and utterly unbalanced. He was tired of batting his head against her well-erected barriers.

"I discovered that I missed Julia. She has always been like a sister to me."

His eyes narrowed at the patent lie.

"You could have requested that she join you in Devonshire," he pointed out with indisputable logic. "No doubt she would have been delighted to mix among the most elite of society."

"For goodness' sakes, Luce, does it matter why I returned?" she demanded in tight tones.

"It does when your return also includes a visit to Calfield Park." He took a step closer, his gaze capturing her own with a relentless intensity.

Her eyes darkened as she crossed her arms. Luce bit back a groan as the soft curves of her bosom were prominently displayed by the deep vee of her robe.

"If you do not wish me to return to Calfield Park, you only have to say so, Luce. I assure you I did not intend to disturb you."

With an effort, he wrenched his hungry gaze from the temptation beneath the soft linen. "I never believed that you did, but I am intrigued at your reasons for seeking me out. When I left London, I was under the impression that you never desired to speak with me again."

Surprisingly, her eyes shimmered with sudden tears before she abruptly turned from his searching gaze.

"I told you . . . I was concerned."

With his heart racing, Luce reached out to grasp her shoulders and relentlessly turned her to face him. He had not been mistaken about the tears. His hand moved of its own accord to gently cup her face.

"Kate."

"What?"

"Tell me. Why?"

She gave a shake of her head. "Please, go away, Luce."

"Did you regret the way we parted?"

"I . . . that's ridiculous."

Luce gave a humorless laugh, nearly driven mad by the sweetly familiar scent of her. Dear heavens, he could drown in that tantalizing aroma.

"I suppose it is," he said in self-mockery. "Just wishful thinking I suppose."

She stilled at his revealing words. "What did you say?"

His lips twisted. "Do not give me that wide-eyed look, Kate. You know how desperately you bewitched me. Did you think I possess no heart? That I walked away without another thought of how you made me laugh, how you made me enjoy your ridiculous adventures, how you fit into my arms as if you had been created just for me?" He gave a disgusted shake of his head. "For God's sake, I thought we were at the very least friends."

She flinched as if she had been slapped. "We are friends."

He gave a humorless laugh. "Then heaven help your enemies."

"I am sorry that you were forced to sell your business—"

"Dammit, this is not about my bloody business, or dowries, or crumbling estates," he interrupted angrily. "It is about us. Are you sorry you forced me out of your life?"

He felt the shudder that raced through her body. "I had to."

His hand moved to tangle in the satin softness of her hair. "Of course. A brief flirtation and then on to the next adventure."

"No," she whispered. "It was not like that."

"Oh yes, I was also the scheming, conniving lecher who was determined to seduce you back to an engagement you detested."

A tear slid down her cheek. "I wanted you to leave because . . ."

"Yes?"

"Because I could no longer pretend that I was not

falling in love with you. And to be honest, I could not bear a broken heart."

He froze in disbelief. "What did you say?"

"I think you heard me."

"You love me?"

She abruptly struggled to free herself. "Please just go away, Luce."

"Never," he swore, his arms wrapping about her wriggling form to haul her firmly against his body. After days of black despair, she was not moving an inch from his embrace. Dropping kisses upon her face, he allowed a wary joy to slowly fill his heart. "My God, I have ached for you for weeks. You have haunted my dreams, distracted my days. I cannot sleep or work or even eat. Every time I close my eyes, I can still smell you. And I have called for my carriage a dozen times to come and bring you home where you belong, only to realize that I could not force you to want to be with me."

A choked moan escaped her lips. "Luce?"

He captured her lips in a deep searching kiss before pulling back to regard her with a stern expression

"And do not dare accuse me of wanting you back for your damn dowry. For all I care you can tell your father to toss his money down the nearest well. All I want is you."

Her lips curved into a tremulous smile. She looked amused and bemused and utterly adorable.

"But what of your estate?"

Luce experienced a brief pang of guilt that he had ever considered taking this woman for the sole purpose of acquiring her wealth.

"I told myself nothing was more important than ensuring the future of my family and estate. And I was quite prepared to take the easy path to do so.

Oh, I tried to convince myself I was committing a great sacrifice to marry wealth, but it was no more than an excuse to avoid making the difficult choices. It was not until you refused to offer your trust that I realized I was behaving no better than my parents. I desired someone else to solve my troubles rather than facing them on my own."

"And now?"

He slowly smiled. "Now I accept that whatever sacrifice I may make to restore my estate, none could be greater than marrying some maiden who is not you. No one could ever replace you in my heart." He gazed deep into her wide eyes. "I love you, Miss Kate Frazer. I want to spend the rest of my life with you."

Without warning, she threw her arms about his neck and pressed herself even closer to his hard form. Luce clutched her tiny body, his senses filled with her warm sweetness.

"I love you," she said simply.

Luce briefly wondered if his heart might actually burst from sheer happiness.

"But what of your desire for daring adventures and independence?" he forced himself to ask the question that still haunted him.

She offered him a brilliant smile. "I have discovered that a life of endless adventures can be as dull as one of endless duty."

"No more adventures?"

"Oh, I did not say that," she corrected, with a glint in her eyes. "I still want to experience new delights. Perhaps as a roguish pirate, you might have a few suggestions?"

Luce gave a low growl as he pressed her against his trembling form. The delights he conjured were enough to make his knees weak and his head spin.

"You are sure? I have nothing to offer but my name and a decidedly uncertain future."

"Oh, yes."

With a slow tenderness, he explored her lips, barely able to believe this extraordinary woman. He had sought a fortune, and he had found it in her love.

"You came home," he whispered against her mouth.

"No, I came to you," she retorted.

"We will rebuild Calfield Park together," he promised as he gently nuzzled her cheek. "For us. For our family."

She reached up to cup his face in gentle hands. "It sounds like a wonderful adventure."

He smiled deep into her eyes as he pressed her slight frame even closer.

"An adventure that will last the rest of our lives."

EPILOGUE

As far as weddings went, this one would be considered an extravagant, spectacular success.

Oh, the entire success could not be attributed to the small church, which was beautifully festooned with flowers, candles, and the few fortunate guests who had been allowed a much sought-after invitation. Nor solely upon the bride, who stood at the altar in a shocking crimson gown, her countenance flushed with happiness. And certainly not upon the vicar, who had once again liberally quenched his thirst from the silver flask he kept concealed beneath his robes.

Weddings by tradition included beautiful churches, glowing brides, and vicars who felt the need to succor their nerves with a swig of brandy.

No. The success could be attributed to the groom.

A groom who arrived near three hours early and who swore before God and man to love, honor, and endow his bride with everlasting adventures through all eternity . . .

ABOUT THE AUTHOR

Debbie Raleigh lives with her family in Missouri. Her next Regency romance, *The Wedding Clause*, will be published in June 2005. Debbie loves to hear from readers, and you may write to her c/o Zebra Books. Please include a self-addressed stamped envelope if you wish a response.

<u>BOOK YOUR PLACE ON OUR WEBSITE</u> AND MAKE THE <u>READING CONNECTION!</u>

We've created a customized website just for our very special readers, where you can get the inside scoop on everything that's going on with Zebra, Pinnacle and Kensington books.

When you come online, you'll have the exciting opportunity to:

- View covers of upcoming books
- Read sample chapters
- Learn about our future publishing schedule (listed by publication month *and author*)
- Find out when your favorite authors will be visiting a city near you
- Search for and order backlist books from our online catalog
- Check out author bios and background information
- Send e-mail to your favorite authors
- Meet the Kensington staff online
- Join us in weekly chats with authors, readers and other guests
- Get writing guidelines
- AND MUCH MORE!

Visit our website at
http://www.kensingtonbooks.com